BRED FOR LOVE

A ROYAL REBELLION

BOOK THREE

by

Revella Hawthorne

Copyright © 2015 by SJ Himes
"Revella Hawthorne"
All rights reserved.

Edited by Amanda Coolong

Cover design by Kellie Dennis at Book Cover By Design
http://www.bookcoverbydesign.co.uk

No part of this book may be reproduced in any form or by any electronic or mechanical means including information storage and retrieval systems, without permission in writing from the author. The only exception is by a reviewer, who may quote short excerpts in a review.

This book is a work of fiction. Names, characters, places, and incidents either are products of the author's imagination or are used fictitiously. Any resemblance to actual persons, living or dead, events, or locales is entirely coincidental.

If you are reading a pirated version or a copy of this book that you did not purchase yourself, or was not gifted/loaned to you through allowable and legal means, then please keep in mind that you have effectively stolen this ebook. That means you have taken money directly from the author, making it harder for the author to continue to write.

Please purchase your own copy, and remember to review.
Revella Hawthorne

http://www.sjhimes.com

CONTENTS

Dedication

Prologue

Chapter One

Chapter Two

Chapter Three

Chapter Four

Chapter Five

Chapter Six

Chapter Seven

Chapter Eight

Chapter Nine

Chapter Ten

Chapter Eleven

Chapter Twelve

Epilogue

To Be Continued

About the Author

Other Books by Revella Hawthorne

DEDICATION

I want to dedicate this book to the fans of the series. Honestly, all of you keep me going. A huge thank you to the members of the Mpreg Book Rec group on Facebook. The support and interest you have all shown in the series is what helps keep me going.

I almost didn't finish this book on time. Severe health issues, living arrangement problems, and then moving 1400 miles away from hearth and home to start over put me so far behind that it is a miracle this book is done.

A clean slate is what I needed, and hopefully the stories in my head will benefit the most.

Thank you to Andrea. For everything. Literally, everything.

To Kellie, for the artwork--you leave me breathless with your talent.

Amanda C., for your patience and time.

To friends and family, for believing in me–

Thank you.

PROLOGUE

At the end of all things...

SCREAMS RIPPED apart the expectant silence.

The men waiting outside in the narrow hall all jumped, and the oldest of them gripped the youngest man's shoulder, holding him up just as much as imparting comfort. There was no power, their battle fought earlier having knocked everything down but what the generator was running in the makeshift operating room. They were too tired to pace, too drained emotionally and mentally to do more than flinch every time the precious life in the next room cried out in pain.

"Please, let them live," whispered the youngest, eyes drawn tight, sweat dripping down his face to blend with his tears of frustration and fear. The silver at his temples belied his age, and the lines long his eyes were deepened by grief. "Please, by the grace of the Saints and the Blood of Our Line, let them live...."

A wail, thin and hopeless. The second man swore viciously and spun, punching the wall, the sound of something breaking filling the empty quiet that fell just as suddenly. The oldest barely reacted, swallowing, the youngest grew taut as cable, and vibrated in horrific tension. Two of the three people he loved most in this world were in there now, fighting to bring a fourth into the world.

The door behind them creaked open, a bare sliver of light spilling into the darkness where they waited. The youngest spun, tottering as he almost fell over, and he anxiously approached the light, hoping even as he despaired. The oldest, gray-haired and used to death, watched impassively, accepting of whatever outcome. The second man gripped the youngest's shoulder, keeping him upright.

"Are they..." he swallowed, and tried again, asking the form standing in the doorway, the light haloed behind the figure making features impossible to discern.

"Edward, is Percy...Is Percy alive? The baby?"

CHAPTER ONE

ALL NEW THINGS BEGIN WITH HOPE

Percy

"HOLD ON!" Reynard shouted, taking the corner too fast, the left side wheels coming up off the ground. Tires squealed, and Edward pulled Percy closer to his side. The sleek car roared forward, the city streets not as narrow the further they got from Mason's neighborhood.

The deception must have been discovered. Barely thirty minutes had passed since they left Mason's townhouse. The two black cars behind them were as expensive as the one they were in, and were so close on their tail Percy feared they were about to be rear-ended. Percy squeezed his eyes shut and clung to Edward. The speed, the sharp turns, the blaring of horns from other vehicles all left Percy screaming in terror.

A hard thump almost sent Percy to the floor. Edward shouted at Reynard, holding Percy tightly to his chest, and another harsh acceleration pressed them to the seat.

"Saint's blood, Reynard, if the guards don't kill us first, this chase will! End it!"

"I'm trying not to kill the guards!" Reynard shouted back, sending them around another corner.

"It's obvious they don't care about whether or not they kill us or anyone else on the streets! End this now, and get us out of here!"

"Yes, my prince!" The car shot forward again, but then Reynard did something, and Percy moaned, desperately trying not to get sick, as they spun. Percy felt the car stop, and Reynard got out. There was a tremendous bang and thump off to the right, followed by a loud cacophony of gunshots. Shouts, screams, orders to halt, followed by some more shots.

Silence.

Percy opened his eyes. It was quiet, the engine purring. The city street was empty, pristine in front of them, and Percy lifted his head, trying to spot Reynard.

Edward grabbed his head, and pressed his face to his hard chest. "Don't look, Percy. Keep your head down."

"Is he…is Reynard…?"

"I'm fine, Perseus," Reynard said, getting back in the car and shutting the door. The scent of ozone and something metallic filled the car, and Reynard buckled his belt.

Reynard drove, fast but not as fast as before. Edward let his head up, and Percy leaned on the front seat, worried, but Reynard looked fine. The captain gave him a smile, and jerked his chin, and Percy sat back.

There was no way he was asking what happened to the guards pursuing them. He could guess, and he had no wish to be sick in the car thinking about it.

Edward gathered him close again, and Percy snuggled on his lap. Percy put a hand on Edward's leg, and he frowned, pulling it back up.

He had blood on his hand. Edward was bleeding.

Percy

A FLUTTER. A simple, tiny, hesitant movement, but it was enough for Percy to catch his breath, and hold very still, hoping to feel it again. His hand smoothed down his borrowed cotton shift, the swell of his abdomen still so new to him. He waited, hoping, but his child fell back into slumber and grew quiet.

"Perseus! I need those bandages!" Reynard shouted from the other room, and Percy jumped, remembering why he was in the bathroom to begin with. He grabbed the stack of white bandages from under the sink, and ran back to the front of the cottage.

Edward was naked from the waist down, a small pillow over his groin for Reynard's sake, since the former captain was kneeling at the blood prince's feet where he sat on an old couch. Edward's thigh was bleeding, his sutures from the gunshot injury and the resultant surgery ripped in several places. Blood ran down the thick column of his thigh onto the couch, and Percy nearly tripped over his own feet at the sight. Luckily he was close enough to Reynard all the captain needed to do was reach out and take the bandages from his hand.

"Little one, please breathe," Percy shook his head at his master's voice, and gave him a sheepish smile. Edward was watching him, dark eyes glittering. "Come sit with me."

Percy took Edward's outstretched hand, settling beside him on the couch as Reynard wiped blood from the incisions.

Fresh blood welled up to take its place, and Percy turned away, burying his head in Edward's firm shoulder. A hand came to rest in his hair, and tousled the long strands. He kept meaning to ask for some shears so he could cut his hair, but Edward's delight in the length stayed him every time.

Edward's shoulder was warm under his cheek, and Percy melted into his strength. Edward was speaking to Reynard while the other man went about repairing the damage Edward had done to his leg during his escape.

"Do you think Mason made it out alright?" Edward was asking, referring to the older blood prince's assistance in Edward's escape.

Percy lost track of the long hours since Edward boldly walked out of the hospital, dressed as Mason, fooling everyone in the royal guard, the press, and the public. Where the public believed him to be under protection of the guards for a botched assassination attempt, he'd actually been under arrest for going against his father's commands and refusing to surrender Percy. It was the brothers' remarkable similarities to each other that let Edward get away from the hospital and the guards...but it meant Mason had to stay in his place, and Percy was worried for the older blood prince.

The deception didn't last long, but it held long enough for them to get out of the city. The car chase was the last they saw of the guards, and Reynard had taken them through hours' worth of side streets and country roads until they made it to the royal highway. A few hours on the highway, and they stopped to tend to Edward's leg when the bleeding failed to stop.

"Your brother has made it out of worse binds than the one

he's in now," Reynard answered, and Percy peeked to watch as Reynard put neat, tiny stitches in place along the worst of the torn areas in Edward's leg. Reynard was fast and efficient, and the flesh was swiftly returned to a semblance of order.

"He saved you. He helped us, and he didn't have to," Percy whispered, nibbling on his lip. He had quickly grown fond of the irreverent and mercurial middle son of King Henry the Third. When they first met, Mason alternated between frightening Percy with his too intense regard and teasing his master, but his warm welcome and stalwart support during their ill-fated return to the capital was the only reason the three of them were all alive and together. Percy was terrified that Prince Mason was paying dearly for helping them escape.

A thumb freed his lip from his teeth, and Percy kissed Edward's digit as his head was tilted up, to see Edward's dark, shiny eyes gazing at him with affection.

"I'm worried, too," Edward confessed, sighing, shifting on the couch in discomfort. Whether emotional, physical, or both, Percy wasn't sure. "Mason has always held himself apart, even when we were children. He showed us all only what he wanted us to see. Sarcastic, witty, occasionally cruel. But never outright dishonest, and he never shies from harsh truths. Out of all seven of my siblings, I have always been fondest of him."

"He loves you," Percy said, certain of this fact. He may have doubted Prince Mason in the beginning, wary of his actions and intent, but when Edward was arrested and Percy and Reynard came to Mason for help, the middle prince was unerring in his determination to see Edward and Percy reunited. When Reynard proposed the plan to have Mason substitute himself for Edward, the blood prince hadn't even hesitated.

Reynard wrapped Edward's leg, cushioning the new sutures and securing the thick bandages around Edward's thigh. The padding was thicker, and would hopefully ease some of his lover's pain.

"Done, my prince," Reynard spoke, standing from his kneeling position. He went to their bags piled along the wall and fetched a new pair of black pants for Edward to wear. Percy scrambled up from the couch, trying to lend his prince a hand but Reynard gently nudged him back. Reynard leaned over and pulled Edward upright with a single arm, and held the prince until he was steady. Reynard handed Percy the pants, and he hurriedly assisted Edward into them while Reynard kept him upright.

"We need to go," Edward warned. "We've been here too long."

"Agreed," Reynard said, stepping back as Percy helped Edward into his boots. He was no longer wearing Mason's clothing—they managed to help Edward change them out for an outfit that couldn't be matched to what he was wearing when he escaped the hospital.

The bullet had punched through his right upper thigh, nicking the femoral artery, and ripping a decent sized hole out the back of his leg as it exited. Edward could walk, but the wound was still too fresh, that any movement placed him in danger of reopening the artery. Finding a cabin locked up for the winter season just off the highway they'd taken from Cassia City was a stroke of luck. Reynard's first aid skills were vital in helping Edward, and Percy was incredibly thankful the captain was on their side.

Percy hovered, hands on his lower belly, fingers linked over the swell where his babe slept. Percy had been relieved when they found the cabin, but Reynard's caution and Edward's impatience made it clear that Percy wouldn't be getting the rest he so desperately needed. They had to keep moving, surely the guards couldn't be that far behind.

Reynard moved around Percy, heading for the back of the cabin, but he paused long enough to lift a hand to Percy's cheek and wipe away a tear he didn't know he was shedding. "Perseus, everything will be fine."

Percy nodded, and Reynard moved on down the hall. Edward's hand on his shoulder made him turn and Percy snuggled immediately into his embrace, savoring the warmth in the hard muscles and strong arms that held him so tight.

He risked a glance up, and Edward wasn't looking at him, but down the hall, where it sounded like Reynard was raiding the supplies in the linen closet. They had plenty from Mason's place, the blood prince's generosity more than enough to see them through the next few days, but Percy was quickly coming to understand that Reynard was never too prepared for anything.

"Edward?" Percy flushed, still not used to calling his master and lover by his given name when there were others nearby to hear. It was a recent development, and while Reynard had known all along that Edward allowed Percy liberties in how they spoke to each other, that still couldn't erase his nervous tension that someone would one day overhear and object. He was working on his bravery, but a part of him feared he'd never be as brave as Edward or their baby needed.

Edward blinked, his intense stare dissipating, and he looked down at Percy, smiling. The kiss he gave him was soft and sweet, and Percy melted into him, seeking more.

Edward

PERCY TASTED sweet and welcoming, and Edward sipped from his lips, taking his time. His little mate's eager submission to his touch made his blood heat, despite the pain and weakness he was suffering due to his injury. If they weren't being hunted and if Reynard wasn't a few feet away, Edward would love to sit back down on the old couch and ravish every single delectable inch of Percy's body.

Edward eased away, and he smiled at the dazed and aroused expression in his mate's ice-blue eyes. Such beautiful and arresting eyes, eyes that held innocence and strength, compassion and determination. Eyes that made his breath catch, his body sing with captivated lust and interest the first time he saw them at Heritage.

The fear Percy's eyes usually showed the world was fading away, day by day, and every time Edward told Percy how much he loved him. His brother Mason once observed that Percy was different, that love was curing his fears. Edward hope it was true, since the days and weeks ahead were going to hold plenty to fear.

Edward couldn't resist, and he palmed the gentle bump in Percy's abdomen where their babe rested. Percy shivered, and curled into him, one of his small hands laying over Edward's. They both held still, as if listening, but Edward thought it was still too early for their child to be active. One day soon though, and they would be able to feel the movements of the life growing inside.

"My prince, we must go," Reynard said, his voice breaking them from their silent communion. Percy leaned on him, and Edward took his weight. Percy was doing so well, but Edward worried for his mate. Percy had little stamina, his life up until the previous month naught but time in a windowless cell, and then weeks of morning sickness left Percy lacking when it came to endurance. Though he was nearly insatiable when aroused, leaving Edward completely depleted and exhausted.

"I know," Edward murmured, Reynard walking past them with a linen laundry bag over his broad shoulder, full of purloined supplies form the cabin. Edward put an arm around Percy, and refused to show how even Percy's slight weight put strain on his leg. The day he was unable to tend to Percy was the day he died.

Reynard went to the front door, opening it a hair, peeking out into the darkness. It was late at night, and the distant lights of cars on the Royal Highway could be seen through the trees. Cold air swept in and Percy shivered, and Edward blocked him from the worst of the wind as the captain disappeared into the darkness of the front garden. Edward listened, keeping himself from tensing so as not to scare Percy.

When he heard the engine turn over and headlights flooded the front, Edward relaxed. He moved forward, towing Percy behind him, just as Reynard returned. "In the back, please," Reynard instructed, slipping past them and picking up half of their bags.

Edward guided Percy out the door and down the front

steps towards the driveway, his brother's car dark and sleek in the shadows, the doors and rear hatch open. Edward gently pushed Percy ahead of him and in the spacious backseat, sliding in behind his mate and shutting the doors. Reynard put their bags in the rear and returned to the cottage, grabbing the last of their gear and shutting out the lights, making sure to lock the door behind him.

Moments later they were pulling away from the cabin, the car gliding through the trees along the stone drive, heading back for the highway.

They came to the exit ramps a few minutes later, and they sat at the intersection. The road headed off in into the darkness of the mountains, the other direction back to the capital. Along the road out into the far country lay the distant border of Elysian, one of the most powerful and technologically advanced countries on the planet. It was from that country that Edward's late mother, the deceased Queen of Cassia came from, and nestled in idyllic forests along the River Styx was one of the many estates she left to Edward when she passed. Elysian came in close second to Cassia in terms of wealth and power, but the most important part about Elysian at that moment for Edward was that the neighboring country outlawed and eradicated all slavery practices and customs two decades prior.

Percy would be considered a person, sentient, real, with rights and value as a man the second he stepped over that border. Once protected by Elysian law, no one, not even Edward, would be able to deny Percy his basic rights as a person, nor deny him rights to his unborn child.

Edward's rights to him would only be recognized if they

were there with diplomatic status, under the auspices of Edward's birthrights as a Blood Prince of Cassia. With the three of them marked as fugitives and potentially traitors for defying the King, the claims of ownership Edward held over Percy would be meaningless. Not even the rank of consort would mean anything without the endorsement of the Cassian throne if Edward was declared a traitor.

Edward met Reynard's eyes in the rearview mirror. There was no doubt the captain knew all of this as well. It was common knowledge that Elysian stopped engaging in the slave trade, and that no sales or trading of genetically modified humans with Cassia was allowed. It was taught in primary school as part of world history classes.

Reynard's eyes darted to Percy, where the young breeder was cuddled along Edward's side, almost asleep, eyes heavy and breathing slow and relaxed. Reynard looked back to him, and Edward nodded.

"Head east, Abe. Elysian and freedom." Edward said, and the car took the ramp, aimed for the eastern horizon.

CHAPTER TWO

Mason

PAIN WAS an ever-present reminder that just because he was royal, that didn't mean he was impervious to harm. And yet, as each blow fell, each twist to resisting joints and every searing touch of hot metal to tender flesh, Mason was reminded of not all the times his father beat him as a child, but of the missions gone awry in the army, in years long past.

Missions where he ended up held prisoner by the enemies of the Crown, tortured, beaten, assaulted, and eventually rescued, but not after days and weeks held in cells and dungeons infested with rats and roaches, mud and swampy water. Yet it was those days of misery that he yearned for, because it was in those distant times he had hope...hope of rescue, reprieve.

There was no rescue for this prince of Cassia, not from this enemy. Not when the pain came from the hands of his own father.

King Henry the Third, Monarch and Supreme Ruler of the Kingdom of Cassia had a mean left hook. He wielded that red-hot poker like he stoked fires all day long, and the silk ties he utilized to twist Mason into unbearable positions would have done a non-consensual practicing sadist proud.

Mason was jolted from his memories of one particularly bad mission in the jungle of a southern shithole of a country when he hit the floor with a meaty slap. Stars clouded his eyes when his head hit the stone floor, but he still found relief as the silk ties around his wrists and ankles loosened and fell away. Blood returned to his extremities in a painful rush, but he lacked the strength to massage his arms and legs to ease the sensation.

"Shall I send for the physician, my king?" a bland, even voice asked somewhere out of view of Mason's bleary vision.

"I doubt I injured anything vital. Leave him there, he can drag himself to bed once he comes around," his father replied, and Mason could see his booted feet pass in front of his line of sight, heading for the door. "If he wishes to cooperate after this lesson, do let me know."

"Yes, Sire," the servant replied, following King Henry from the room, leaving Mason alone on the cold stone floor in the cell passing for his new room in the palace. The door shut and the lock turned over with a final snick, and silence descended in the small room.

He was in the petitioner's quarters inside the Old Palace, the structure once called home by the great King Airric at the birth of the Cassian Dynasty two thousand years ago. The modern palace seen by the world surrounded and protected the ancient castle at its core, keeping the original seat of their power safe from the erosions of time and prying eyes.

Mason and his brothers used to play in the vaulted halls and stone walled rooms as children, imagining they were stalwart knights battling scores of savages and monsters, saving their kingdom over and over again, returning conquering heroes. It was a weird twist to Fate that Mason now found himself locked away in a room he used to retreat to as a young man, seeking asylum from the increasing demands of his duties as a blood prince and the second born son of the king.

Here, in the Old Palace, no one would hear him scream when the pain got too much too bear.

Mason cautiously pushed himself upright, the room spinning before his brain settled, and he spit out grit and blood to the floor. He leaned back against the wall, eyeing the distant pitcher of water on the nightstand, wondering if today would be the day he lacked the strength to get up and drink some of the cool fluid.

Maybe he should just give up. There was no point in continuing to bait his father with his refusal to speak. Not that he knew anything for certain to tell his father about where Edward and his shy mate were hiding or where they were heading. Though there was one person Mason knew better than anyone other than his brothers in this world, and that person was Abelard Toussaint Reynard, minor baron and once honored captain in the Royal Guard. Mason knew the way Reynard thought, the way he would prepare and act, and if Mason were to make an educated guess, Reynard and Edward would be taking Percy over the nearest border with Elysian.

Percy was a slave, a breeder, and once he asked for asylum in Elysian, he would be safe.

The King and his men were focusing the search on Hartgrove, Edward's massive country estate, and the routes through the mountains between Cassia City and the estate. Edward's fondness for his country home was well-known, and if Mason hadn't known Eddie and Reynard so well, he would think the trio would retreat to that place of safety and power as well. It was defensible and Edward knew the area better than the locals.

Mason understood one thing that the King didn't.

Edward, and Reynard, both loved the young breeder. Maybe not in the same way or for the same reasons, but that love was real. And that love meant they would do anything to keep Percy safe. Even if safety meant sacrificing any claims they had over the beautiful and exceptional breeder.

It was that thought that made Mason push aside any inclinations of giving up. He would survive his father's fury, escape, and do what he should have done years ago. Expose the king for the monster he was, rip apart the secrets of the Cassian Dynasty, and maybe find some measure of peace in his otherwise joyless existence. It was love that kept him going all these years as his father, with casual cruelty and vindictive precision, stripped Mason of all he held dear and forced him into a stilted half-life, a façade of perfection that grew into a torture and prison with each passing day. Love kept him alive, and kept him from falling apart as he pretended to be the rapscallion second son and loyal prince.

His penchant for surviving was both gift and curse, ever since that fateful day he loitered at his dying mother's bedside and learned a truth that could shatter the greatest royal dynasty to ever rule on this world.

Those he loved were already past the king's reach. His silence could no longer be guaranteed by the threat to their lives. His sisters, those spoiled and hollow creatures sold in marriage to wealthy men, were beyond harm at their husbands' sides. Edward was safe, Malcolm was a lost cause, and the other …

King Henry could no longer force Mason's cooperation by

threatening the life of the man he loved.

Abe Reynard was in the wind, and far more dangerous than the young innocent he once was, vulnerable to a king's wrath. Now all Mason had to do was set free the truth, even if that meant he died trying.

HE WAS sleeping. Or trying. Pain made it hard to relax. If not for the lateness of the hour he wouldn't dare attempt to sleep. His father was too busy being entertained by his ministers and the Court to come and beat him at this hour, so he was guaranteed some peace until morning.

"Mason?"

He frowned at the harsh whisper, almost too loud to be counted as such, as if the speaker had little experience with such foolish things. Only one person he knew of who was so atrocious at being quiet. And who liked to wander at midnight to places she had no business being, even for the queen-in-waiting.

"Come to gloat at my downfall, Arianna?" he called to the door, the oak panel solid but for a small hole filled with iron bars near the top. He rolled over on the thin pallet that counted as a bed, and squinted through the shadows. The light in the hall was bright enough for him to see the top of his sister-in-law's head, her typically tamed curls fuzzy and piled high, bouncing as she tried to see through the window in the door.

He laughed, the motion hurting his ribs and shoulders, but it felt good to make a sound that wasn't wholly pain-filled. If only the rest of the world could see the future Queen of Cassia as she was now, bored and alone at night, dressed in her nightgown and wandering through the palace like a recalcitrant preteen anxious to avoid going to bed.

"Oomph! Oh, bloody hell, why are these blasted chairs so damn heavy?" Mason heard her swear through the door, and he thought it likely that the guard was either dead, knocked unconscious, or absent to miss the racket Arianna was making in the hall. A clang, then the door shuddered, and suddenly Ari's makeup smudged and tired face appeared in the window.

"Oh! So it's true then, King Henry has finally done it. He always said he was going to lock you up and throw away the key one of these days, but I never thought I'd actually see him do it," she quipped, the light bright enough for him to see her white smile, her hands clutching the bars.

"Such a stellar wit for so exalted a personage," Mason growled, painfully sitting up. He blinked against the light that came through from the hall, shielding his eyes until he adjusted. He heard Ari gasp, and he was about to laugh, expecting her to fall on her butt in the hallway, but all he got was the sound of sniffling.

"Are you crying?" he asked, wary even though they were separated by the door. Crying females always made him want to run away. There wasn't much that scared him, but a female and tears did it every time. And he couldn't escape right now, he was locked up in a medieval cell.

He was again thankful that his psychotic bitch of a wife wasn't the type to cry, staying disturbingly dry-eyed even when faced with the most devastating of news. Nothing made that woman flinch, and sentimental she was not. For instance, she had yet to come visit him in his comfy prison cell, and he had no doubt she knew he was here. She just didn't care. She was most likely hanging on his father's arm, the bitch.

"Why, for Saint's sake, are you crying?"

And she was. Big tears ran down her cheeks, a hand over her mouth, and she stared at him, eyes tracing over his bare shoulders and chest, obviously seeing the scores across his flesh from fist and scorching hot poker. He'd had worse, truly, but to the relatively sheltered eyes of Princess Arianna, he must be horrendous looking indeed.

"Mason, tell me what is going on! This instant!" she demanded, furiously wiping away her tears, her angry response coming out to play when confronted by unpleasant news. "You've been hurt! WHY? King Henry said you were merely in here for a few days as punishment for letting Eddie sneak out, and he'd let you out once you told him where Eddie and his little pet were! What the hell is going on?!"

He could continue to cover for this bastard of a father as he had for the last several years, or should he reveal the truth? It was the spoiled, erratic, and temperamental princess on the other side of the door who'd been misled the most by the King and his machinations, and she had no clue. Perhaps the truth would out, after all. Their family and kingdom were about to shatter, and Mason was so tired of carrying the lies that hid the truth around with him every-damn-day.

The only member of their family right now who was stain-free was Edward, and he was blissfully unaware. His life was about to change, for better or worse, and he felt a twinge of regret. Perhaps Eddie would be better off if he stayed silent. But the dishonor of their father's actions left them all marred, and those actions drove every decision made by the King since that fateful day the late Queen passed. With Eddie gone and Abe out of the king's reach, it was now or never.

He stood, pausing until he could trust his feet to remain steady under him, and he slowly made it to the door. He gripped the bars, face mere inches from hers, and he met her confused gaze.

"Shall I tell you a story, dear sister? It is no fairy tale, there are no heroes...." Arianna's eyes went round, and she nodded, captivated by the intensity in his voice. "It begins with a young princess from the faraway land of Elysian, sent to marry the young crown prince of Cassia, many long years ago. She brought with her a curse, and there was no true love to break it...."

Percy

EDWARD'S ARM around his waist was heavy, and his bladder was complaining. Percy squirmed, and wiggled his way out from under his master's arm, sliding from the bed, bare feet finding the chill floor. He gasped, but dared the rest of the expanse between bed and bathroom, darting in and shutting the door. He flicked on the light, glad that the light in here worked, if nothing else. Even when he lived at Heritage in his windowless cell, his space was clean and the commodities worked reliably. Here in this run down shack Reynard led them to, Percy was afraid one of his toes was going to be gnawed on by a rat or a cockroach.

 Percy lost track of how long they'd been on the road. The comfortable car Mason gave them was left in a place Reynard called a "chop shop", and in return they were given the keys to an older vehicle, something Edward called an SUV. It was big and bulky, and the last row of seats was missing, but Edward filled it with blankets and told him to rest. The hours spent on the road was made bearable by the grocery bag of books Edward gave him one morning, titles Percy had never even heard of before by unknown authors, and he spent a good portion of the trip oblivious to the passage of time. He would look up on occasion, and watch the scenery as Reynard drove.

 The area closest to Cassia City was an odd mix of large palatial estates belonging to nobles, interspersed with densely populated towns Edward told him were "micro-cities", places where the general populace settled on land not owned by the crown or a noble. Once outside the city limits, every spare patch of earth available was snatched up, and commoners were left with the undesirable bits. Percy asked question after question, Edward patiently explaining the history of Cassia as they went further and further away from the City.

 Centuries ago, the only people allowed to own land had been the royals and those of noble blood, and the land around Cassia City in all directions for several days' worth of travel via horseback was claimed, leaving nothing for the commoners. They were allowed to lease and rent land from the nobility and crown, and whole villages and towns were settled, but everything was still owned by a select few. No one owned the roofs over their heads or the land beneath their feet, and if the owners of the land wanted to evict the tenants, they needed no cause or justification.

Percy listened, shocked on some deep level by what Edward was describing to him, and it was only in the last hundred years that things gradually changed. Individual, non-titled citizens were given the right to own land directly, and while the balance of power never shifted away from the upper classes, a strong middle class of merchants, traders, and entrepreneurs grew rapidly. Edward told him that is was at about the same time genetic engineering and manipulation became viable, and technology as a whole expanded by leaps and bounds, that the laws and systems of the Cassian government and culture began to change.

Percy shook his head, clearing out his busy thoughts. He was weary still, but he made himself use the toilet. He checked the floor around the toilet for creep-crawlies before urinating, and he sighed in relief at the lessening of pressure on his bladder.

Percy leaned on the wall in the small bathroom, wondering if he was brave enough to wander down the hall to the tiny kitchen and get himself some water. He would need to go to the bathroom sooner if he drank now, but he was thirsty, and his brain too busy to sleep. He looked back at the bed, and saw his master still sleeping.

Edward had been tense and on edge the last several days. Percy lost track of time, but with each passing day Edward was tenser, warier, and the words exchanged between Reynard and his master were terse and clipped. Neither man lost his temper, nor did they speak to Percy with anything but care and affection, but the stress they were all under was wearing them down. Reynard was coping best, the former captain obviously accustomed to difficulty. Edward, while no stranger to hard work, was still very used to having servants and a staff take care of his needs, and Percy could see the subtle shifts in how Edward reacted to situations. Paying for things directly, having to ration resources and go out in disguise daily left Edward cranky, for lack of a better word.

Percy was well used to owning nothing, and following orders exactly. Living with minimal belongings, eating when only hungry, and having little clothing was of no bother to Percy, and he did his best to keep from being a burden to either Edward or Reynard. All he did was read, sleep, and ask questions about the world around him when Edward and Reynard needed the distraction from each other's company.

Percy left the bathroom, quietly walking back towards the bed, looking at Edward where he was sprawled on the mattress. Edward must have rolled over on his back while he was in the bathroom, and Edward's naked body was on display, half in shadow.

Tanned skin, body relatively hairless but for a neatly trimmed patch on his groin, and covered in defined muscles, Edward was a sight to see. Thick, wavy black hair and dark brown eyes paired with chiseled cheeks and a string jaw crafted the ideal image of a prince. Edward was handsome, and charming, and sweet, and he made love to Percy with a fierceness that left him breathless.

Percy let his eyes drift, sweeping down Edward's chest, over the planes of his stomach to his groin. Percy's breath hitched, and he licked his lips. He shifted on his feet, and his hole fluttered, clenching slightly before relaxing. Percy moaned, a soft breathy sigh of sound, and he felt a tiny bit of dampening between his ass cheeks. Suddenly he was aroused, his slim cock plumping up and growing, his now-aching hole growing wetter, and his hands trembled with the desire to touch.

He inched closer to the bed, heart tripping, his body wakening in the most delicious way imaginable. Desire always rode him hard, but this time it was coming over him in a spine-tingling rush.

"Edward?" he whispered, reaching out, fingertips trailing across smooth skin and hard muscles. His master's skin was hot to the touch, or perhaps that was him? He was burning, a deep ache settling in at the base of his spine, his internal muscles clamping and releasing, as if Edward was already buried balls deep inside of him. He put the heel of his hand over the swell in his abdomen, and the firmness there where their child grew only made him moan some more. Just the thought, the touch to confirm his body already succored Edward's seed was enough to tip him over the edge into arousal-laced madness.

Somehow he ended up on top of Edward, nipping and whimpering. Edward woke with a gasp that quickly gave way to indulgent chuckles, and Percy found himself flipped, on his back and under his master. Percy spread his legs, opening himself wide, and Edward lowered his hips down between them.

"Hello, my love," Edward murmured, licking at the side of his neck, making Percy groan and squirm, aching and empty. He wanted his master in him, and now. "Do you need something?"

A growing hardness against his hip and the sure, knowledgeable fingers suddenly playing with his wet hole told him Edward knew exactly what he wanted, what he needed.

"Please," he begged, as Edward merely teased his hole and spread his juices around, slicking his crease. "Please fuck me."

"You beg so prettily," Edward husked, kissing him deep and hard, stealing his breath, even as his fingers left and the wide, hard head of his cock nudged at Percy's eager opening. The natural slick his body produced gave Edward more than enough lubrication, and Percy moaned into Edward's mouth as he was steadily and mercilessly impaled on long, thick, hot flesh.

His body opened, muscles caressing and milking the huge cock filling him. Edward kept kissing him, pushing in until he was fully seated, cockhead knocking on the closed entrance to his womb. Edward pushed just a bit harder, and Percy went wild, ripping his mouth away from Edward's and clawing at his shoulders and back. He cried and sobbed, and Edward pulled back, leaving only a few inches, before surging forward again, snapping his hips so he pushed in almost too far. Percy's muscles were strong and resistant, and his body accepted the rough fucking readily.

Edward lifted his shoulders up, bracing his upper torso on his elbows, and he looked down between them, where his hips pistoned between Percy's spread thighs. Percy grabbed his knees and opened himself further, and Edward took advantage of the increased access by thrusting harder, deeper, opening Percy completely. Percy arched into the thrusts, angling his hips so Edward hit him in just the right spot, his chute beginning to tighten as his orgasm approached. Edward groaned, feeling it begin, and took him harder, too an impossible degree.

Wet slaps of flesh and the scent of liquid sex filled the air.

The old bed creaked and complained at the rough use, and Percy gripped the sheets, tearing them as he wrapped his legs around Edward's hips.

Percy's slim cock was now trapped between Edward's abdomen and the baby bump, and Percy squealed at the delicious friction, coming apart instantly in an orgasm that left him shrieking as he came. Hot spurts of his seed shot from his cock, and his chute clamped down on Edward's cock, halting his thrusts immediately. Edward was sucked back in by the powerful muscles that left Percy different from every other soul in the world, giving Edward no options other than to come, and hard.

Edward threw back his head, shouting, eyes clenched tight, sweat pouring down his temples, hands gripping Percy's shoulders as his back bowed. Percy came again when Edward erupted inside him, thick, hot liquid ropes of semen filling Percy's ass, the flow stopping at his sealed womb, making him feel incredibly over-full before the seed began to pulse out around the tight seal his ass had on the hard flesh stretching him wide.

Edward collapsed on top of him, panting hard, sweaty and hot to the touch. Percy gasped at each pulse of seed from his master, Percy's body milking all it could from his prince. He may be pregnant already, but his body still went through the motions of acquiring his partner's seed, and Edward jolted at each hard clench on his cock. He was still hard, moaning and twitching as Percy's body took what it needed from him.

He lost track of how long they were locked together. Edward released his seed in him a handful of times before Percy's body relaxed, its demanding grip easing up enough for

Edward to pull out. They both groaned as the connection was lost, and Edward rolled to his back, pulling Percy with him and on his chest. Percy lay limp and satisfied, Edward's hands tracing over his damp skin and rubbing his hips.

He was wet and damp and cold between his legs where the night air touched the remnants of their passion, but he was too sated to care.

"I love you, Edward," Percy whispered in the dark, pressing a kiss to his lover's chest over his heart.

Edward gently hugged him, and whispered in return, "I love you too, little one."

CHAPTER THREE

Reynard

HE STOOD in the hall, gun in hand, and he smiled at his reaction. He'd awakened to hear Percy screaming, and rushed for the room where his prince and the royal consort slept, heart pounding. He got to the door, and instead of hearing them fighting off royal guards, he caught the tail end of a passionate encounter that left him adjusting a partial erection in his sweatpants. The lovers were rarely quiet, Percy being incredibly vocal and demanding when he was in the throes of passion. Reynard had been subject to their sessions many a time, his duties as royal guard keeping him within sight or sound of his charges at all times, even when they didn't know it, so this was not the first time, nor would it be the last, that he would be able to hear them having sex.

Reynard walked away from the door, and since he was awake, got dressed, intending to do a perimeter sweep around the small cottage. He pulled on his clothes, tucked a firearm at the base of his spine inside his waistband, and a jacket on his way out. He closed the front door quietly, not wanting to alarm his charges. Percy was easily frightened, though his courage was growing with every day that passed, and Edward was hanging on to his composure by a thread. His prince, while used to the pressures of his rank and duties, was at a loss when it came to living away from the comforts of wealth and royalty. Edward was far from spoiled—but his prince was just that—a prince, and accustomed to a certain lifestyle.

Reynard prowled through the cold shadows, the cottage they were occupying on the outskirts of a small micro-city just off the royal highway. The area was partially abandoned, its remaining citizens poor, older, or incapable of moving to one of the larger cities closer to the capital. It was out in the middle of nowhere, with nothing to recommend it to tourists, and so the settlement that developed when the great highways system was first built almost a hundred years ago was steadily losing people to death and time and lack of interest. Over half the houses and businesses were empty, and the streets were pitted and cracked.

The SUV he traded for Mason's sleek beast of a car was hunkered down in the deep shadows next to the small cottage, pointed toward the road for a fast getaway if they were tracked here. They were almost 800 miles from Cassia City, and they had another 1500 miles to go to get to the border with Elysian. As a country, Cassia was one of the largest in the world, occupying a huge portion of the northern half of the largest continent. It was also the longest ruled, single-dynasty monarchy in history, the line of Airric unbroken for two thousand years. Two of his descendants were within shouting distance of him now, and Reynard took the job of protecting Edward, Percy and their unborn babe seriously. It was an honor to serve the Cassian Dynasty, even if some of its members were spoiled brats and fractured souls.

Edward was worth his weight in gold. The youngest blood prince was humble, honest, braver than he had any reason to be, intelligent and even-tempered. He didn't know Edward as well as he did Mason, but then he was only recently assigned to Edward's detail as a captain. Mason, that prince, that man... he knew very well.

Reynard finished his sweep, the nearest sounds of life blocks away and muted. It was quiet, and cold, and the skies above were crystal clear and sparkling, a wide swath of stars filling the horizon end to end.

He leaned against the SUV's hood, crossing his legs at his ankles, hands in his pockets. He watched the sky, and remembered.

A sarcastic, wry smile. Dark eyes, full of passion and fire. And pain. Hair just beginning to be touched by time, a spattering of white at each temple. Golden skin, firm muscles, and a rich, masculine scent that Reynard would never be able to forget.

Forgetting Mason, Blood Prince of Cassia, would be impossible. Almost as impossible as saving him. Reynard was tasked by duty and ...love, to protect Edward and Percy and their babe. He refused to fail. He would never let them down, and while his heart ached fiercely with the need to save Mason, he couldn't abandon his charges to do so. Mason was trapped, by his word and his blood, and the only one who could help him was himself.

Percy

PERCY STAYED behind Edward, one hand clutched in his master's jacket. They were in the market, Reynard a few steps away, arguing with a shady looking man about accommodations for the night. They had left the derelict micro-city behind, and were now days further east. Ten days in total since they had escaped the capital, and they were all feeling it. They were coming up on a portion of the country that was fully wild and untamed forests, sprinkled with small hamlets and tiny towns, and large, sprawling country estates much like Hartgrove. Here the estates were vineyards and orchards, all dormant in the winter months, surrounded by dense old wood forests.

The town they were in was near an estate called Estiary, which Percy thought odd. Edward grew grim, mouth tight, and Reynard looked like he was ready to murder someone, but they needed to stop for supplies, and this town was the last one before a long stretch of wilderness. Percy could tell from the way both men were reacting to the name of the town that something was very wrong, and Percy stayed in Edward's shadow, head down, doing his best to be unobtrusive and forgettable.

"The inn is your best bet, my lord," sniveled the odd man Reynard was speaking to, "the one next to the pub. The Discontent Noble is the pub's name. Can't miss it."

The odd man, thin and whip-like with a narrow countenance and gray overtones to everything from hair to skin, pointed down the length of the market. "The bar and pub are closed until noon, then open for lunch and evening business."

"Thank you," Reynard said, dropping a golden half-piece coin in the man's hand before nodding and walking back towards where he and Edward were waiting next to a wall. The odd man watched them as Reynard walked away, biting the coin before grinning and ducking out of sight in the crowd.

"He was a bit …off," Edward murmured to the captain once he was in earshot. "Will he cause us trouble?"

"Probably, but we haven't got much in the way of options." Reynard jerked his head down the market, and Percy and Edward followed him, Percy between both men. Edward had his arm around his shoulders, and Reynard walked close enough to touch him, their arms occasionally brushing. He felt dwarfed and sheltered between them, and he was thankful he had yet to feel smothered. Reynard continued speaking, voice low, head tilted down to make it harder for them to be overheard. "If we had secure computer access or untraceable cells, this would be easier, but I asked around. This whole village is owned by the local nobleman, and there's only one inn. No apartments for rent or lease, no vacant homes we can take over without being noticed. The estate controls the power, the internet, even the local cell tower, so I believe everything is monitored, nothing secure."

Reynard frowned, glaring back down the length of the market. "So unless you want to rough it in the forest, we have little choice but to stay at the inn."

Percy shivered, thinking back to how uncomfortable it had been a few nights back, sleeping at a rest stop off the highway between towns. He may fit comfortably in the rear of the SUV, but Edward and Reynard were too large to find any decent rest in the vehicle.

"Should we risk staying at a public establishment?" Edward asked, tone curt, arm about Percy's shoulder tightening.

"What if someone sees us and reports us to the authorities?"

"Just having you two walk around in public is too much of a risk, if you're going to be asking that," Reynard snapped, "but since every time I suggest you stay behind with Percy, you claim it's safer if we stay together…"

"Because it is!" Edward hissed, stopping in the middle of the market, glaring over Percy's head at Reynard, who stopped as well. Percy bit his lip and looked nervously between the two big men, wondering if he should worry about ducking. "I may know how to shoot a gun, and throw a punch, but I'm no defense for my mate if we're cornered by the royal guards, and you know it! So yes, we need to stay together, because you are his best chance at surviving this, I'll not have us separated again!"

Reynard's brows went up at that declaration, dark blue eyes calming, and his gaze searching as he looked at the prince. Percy slid his hand to rest on Edward's side, feeling how hard his lover was breathing, how tense he was, so taut he trembled. Edward was beyond stressed.

Reynard stepped so close to Edward that Percy was pressed between them, his back to Edward's chest, Reynard firm and strong along his front. Percy shivered, not entirely certain he disliked where he was, but Edward was ready to snap, so he held very still and waited.

"My prince," Reynard said softly, looking Edward in the eye, forcing Percy to tip his head back at his proximity, "If you trust me to keep your mate safe, even above yourself, then please, please trust that I can care for you both, and that I know what I'm doing. If I say it's safe for us to separate, then trust me. If I say we need to stay together, then we will. In

Court, Palace, and country estate, you know best and are master. Yet out here, in the wilds of the common lands, follow my lead. Do you think you can do that?"

Percy couldn't see Edward's face, but after a moment he felt Edward nod, his tense frame slowly relaxing. Edward put his hands on Percy's shoulders, and turned him from Reynard, pressing his face to his chest. Reynard was still at Percy's back, the heat from both men in the cold winter air comforting and stimulating at the same time. Percy snuggled into Edward, relieved that the tension seemed to be dissipating for now.

Reynard put a hand to the back of Percy's head, tousling his long hair affectionately before stepping away, leaving his back exposed to the cold elements. Edward hugged him for a moment more, but then tugged him to follow after the captain as he cut through the meager crowd in the square.

The sign soon appeared for The Discontent Noble, and Percy giggled at the picture of a finely dressed man sitting on a crooked stool, his beer stein spilling, and a cranky expression on his features. Reynard pointed to a nearby recess in a wall, and Edward guided Percy there, turning them away from any curious eyes of those passing by on the street while Reynard entered the pub.

Percy kissed Edward's jaw, doing it again until Edward gave him a small smile and hugged him close.

Arianna

ARIANNA SMILED down at her son, little Airric suckling from his bottle with a self-righteous determination. He was as demanding as his siblings, yet somehow she knew that though he was youngest, he would be the ringleader in childhood adventures. Only a few months old, and he watched the world with wise eyes, and his cries for changings and feedings were enough to send the nursery staff running to tend to him.

The day was cold, winter blustering outside the palace walls, the weather keeping the Court subdued and in their private quarters. Usually at this time of day Arianna would be with Malcolm, leisurely strolling the halls of the palace, making sure to be seen. Yet the weather and the twisted tale Mason told her days before drove her here, surrounded by her children and nieces and nephews.

Camilla, Mason's wife, was in the far corner, scolding her oldest son of seven years for failing to do something or other, and Arianna frowned, turning her shoulder so she didn't have to watch. Camilla was a horrid woman. She came to the nursery only when her children stepped out of line for some supposed infraction or another. She delighted in disciplining them, or even better, disciplining the tutors and nursery maids instead. Arianna put her foot down when it came to Camilla interfering with her own children. She would be Queen one day—and while she left the daily care to the governesses and maids, Arianna had final say and authority over her children and how they were to be raised. And Camilla was to have zero private interaction with Arianna's children.

She knew she wasn't the ideal mother, but she wasn't just their mother—she was to be Queen. Her life was not her own. Split between her duties as queen-presumptive and mother,

Arianna regretfully lost much of her time as a parent. It was little hardship on the bad days—she didn't regret the diplomatic trip to Elysian when all of her then five children had the chicken pox. On the good days, though, she missed their little smiles, their grasping sticky hands, and their pleas for story time and coloring sessions.

"You better start behaving! What would your father think? Or the King? Are you always going to be a disappointing child?" Camilla scolded, and Arianna frowned. No one but Ari, Malcolm, Camilla, and the king knew where Mason was, and Arianna went cold to her core. Camilla had to know the state her own husband was in and what was happening to him, she must—how could any royal wife abandon her prince? Even a wife as atrocious as Camilla had to realize that without Mason, she was naught but a gaudy decoration amongst those of the blood. Why wasn't she protesting his treatment, or even visiting him?

"Grandpa never comes here! And Daddy isn't home! I don't care what they think, and I don't care what you think! I hate you!" her nephew shrieked at the top of his lungs, and Arianna smirked as the young boy stormed majestically from the nursery, his siblings and cousins cheering from around the room.

Arianna looked out across the room, trying to block out Camilla where she fumed, taking her anger out on the boy's hapless tutor. Her own children, from her oldest child, the future king, young Simon, to her youngest daughter, Selene, and the middle girls, sitting quietly nearby doing their lessons—and then to her nieces and nephews, Camilla and Mason's children. She drank the sight of them in, for once thinking about what would happen if all of this was taken away. What would happen if Mason was right—a part of her was so angry, so mad at him for even suggesting the horrible reality he told her days before—but another part of her, the part of her that loved Cassia, loved her husband, and loved her children—if Mason was right, then she had two choices, and her rarely exercised conscience was demanding to be heard.

Her children, the succession, the crown and throne—all of it hinged on Mason and whether or not he was lying. Because the anger in her heart battled fiercely with fear—she ached from betrayal. Surely she couldn't believe him. Her children, Malcolm's and Mason's children—they were innocent in all of this, yet to them fell the greatest betrayal.

Well, if Mason was to be believed, if his radical story was true, then they weren't his, and her children.....dear God, by the Saint's grace, he must be lying.

"Molly, take him, please," Arianna called to Airric's nurse, who promptly appeared and took the youngest princeling from her arms. She touched his soft cheek and gave him a strained smile, and all but ran from the room. She caught a glimpse of Camilla watching her leave, a frown on her typically dour face, but Arianna ignored her sister-in-law.

She had to find out. Her nerves were unraveling, and she couldn't lose it in front of the children, or Camilla.

She left the nursery, and took off down the hall in the direction of the king's rooms.

"He has to be lying."

Yes, that was it. Mason was lying. He was always causing trouble, always stirring up his brothers, poking his nose where it shouldn't be. He must be lying!

"He is lying, I know it!" Arianna cursed under her breath as she took a corner too fast, her heavy skirts catching on a stone wall, halting her for a moment before she jerked the fabric free. She huffed out an irritated breath, and let go her death grip on her skirts, determined to regain her composure. She could hardly approach the king in a frazzled state. She walked as fast as she could through the maze of halls until she neared her destination.

Arianna swept down the hall outside the king's study, the tall, dark oak doors closed. The long hall was empty, which if the king had been inside then there would be two guards stationed just outside the doors. Arianna looked over her shoulder, and saw no one, so she hurried forward. Asking the king directly if what Mason had told her was true was less attractive than going through his desk and finding the facts for herself.

The doors weren't locked. She opened one, blessing the well-maintained hinges that let her enter silently, and she shut the door behind her. The hearth was cold, the lights out, the only illumination coming through the drawn curtains. King Henry's desk was along the far wall, which meant anyone coming to speak to the king had to cross the whole room while the king watched them, a tactic his majesty used to intimidate petitioners and his ministers.

Skirts rustling over the rugs, Arianna walked to the desk, breathing ragged, an unlady-like sweat building under her dress. If she were caught, she had no idea what the king would do. Being caught by anyone other than him would be simple—but for Malcolm and the king, she outranked everyone in the building, and the blood princesses were all back at their respective homes. Being the future queen came with plenty of protection, but nothing could protect her from King Henry if he decided to punish her for going through his personal belongings.

Not that she knew for certain how he'd react. The king she knew, and the king painted by Mason in the outlandish story he told her a few nights back, were drastically different. The king she knew, while arrogant and demanding, was a devout family man and dedicated ruler, doing his best to keep Cassia and her people at the top of the power scale. There was no country to match Cassia in the whole world, with Elysian, the late queen's home country, being a close second.

So surely that's what Mason's tale was—just a tale, something he concocted to while away his hours spent being punished for letting Eddie disappear. Though why the king and Malcolm would be so upset over a single breeder when there were literally hundreds of them in the country for them to choose from left her equally confused. Mason's explanation for that was equally ludicrous.

King Henry would never let a single minister mess with the affairs of his children, not even the rich and influential Minister of DNA Engineering and Cloning, no matter how much money was involved. There was no way, just no way that King Henry would bow to the wishes of a minister, and persecute a blood prince and legally bonded royal consort, one that if what Mal and Mason both claimed was true, was carrying a Cassian Royal.

It boggled the mind.

That's why she had to find proof—one way or the other. Either Mason was being his typical prick self, or something horrible was happening. Something so horrible that if true, meant that for the last forty years, from the king to her youngest babe, all of them lived a lie.

A lie that drove a father to chase his own son like a common criminal, and in the ultimate irony—the only one of them not weighed down by the broken laws of the king.

She tore through the drawers of the desk that would open, scattering papers here and there. Just thinking about the wretched things that Mason claimed left her composure in tatters.

Tears found their way past her withering control, her hair falling from its immaculate coif. Her skirts were heavy, the corset too tight, and her limbs trembled, and she yanked fruitlessly at the bottom drawer, the old wooden antique momentarily defeating her. It opened with a snap, and she tumbled backwards, falling on her rear with an undignified squawk. The drawers and its contents spilled across the ancient rug, and Arianna struggled to right herself.

Her right hand landed on something cool and hard, and she stopped, looking down and wondering what it was.

A key, as long as her hand, heavy and made of either copper or brass, shiny and old. She peered at it, and the style was reminiscent of a century past. The end of the key held an emblem, and she tilted it back and forth, thinking it was familiar.

It came to her in a rush, and her mouth opened on a silent 'oh'. Arianna climbed to her feet, and stared at the mess on the floor and desk in consternation. She wasn't one for cleaning, and the king could return at any moment. She rushed for the door, tucking her stolen key into her bodice, making sure it was well hidden. It would take Malcolm to find it there.

She made it back out into the hall, and breathed in relief

when she saw no one. Arianna rushed down the hall, and once she hit the main intersection, turned the opposite way she came from originally. There was only place that key would open, with the crest of the Elysian Royal House upon it.

Her Majesty, once Princess Esme of Elysian, and the late Queen of Cassia, dead these last twenty years. It was her key, and since nothing was in the King's possession that spoke of the truth, then Arianna would go to the one place where the lies began.

Maybe with the queen's key she could unlock the truth. It would be just and proper then, since it was a queen whose first and greatest lie condemned them all.

SHE WAS breathless, more from the possibilities than the fast walk through the palace. The late queen's solarium was as it was the day she died, furniture covered, the books and trinkets and the still present scent of day lilies and roses hanging in the air. It was dust free, as it should be, the servants instructed to clean and little else.

Arianna hurried through the outer sitting area, heading for the door that would take her to the inner sanctum. The queen's private bedroom, traditionally where the wife of the king slept when she wasn't required in her husband's bed. Such practices died out with the late queen, and Arianna had no intention of sleeping somewhere other than beside her husband. Besides, she had plenty of children...

Her stomach churned. She stumbled at the door to the old

queen's room, one hand on the panel. The key in her other, staring down at it, dreading. It was on the other side of this door that she might learn the truth.

Her children would always be hers, and nothing could take from her or change how she felt about them. Yet it was their parentage that was still in question, and so was the line of inheritance. It was the throne and their futures as royals of the Blood that would be taken from them, and all it would take was the truth.

Arianna approached the final door, the ancient key heavy in her hand. She inserted it into the lock, and after some effort, the lock turned, the door opening with a faint snick. She left the key in the door, and with one hand, pushed it wide. It groaned on its hinges, complaining, dust kicking up as the wood scraped over the uncleaned rug.

Darkness. The room was fully shuttered, the air stagnant. Dust floated in the air, and her sinuses burned with the desire to sneeze. Putting a hand over her nose and mouth, Arianna took one step in and looked around for a light switch. She found it, and flipped it on, and lights fluttered around the room. A few bulbs popped and went out, but enough stayed on she could see.

Arianna took in the late queen's private room. While the outer sitting area had been cleaned, it was obvious this room hadn't been touched in decades. Probably not since the queen died in her bed, just ten feet from where Arianna stood now. Her blood chilling despite the stifling atmosphere, Arianna shivered in morbid dismay. She had no idea where to look.

What was it that Mason said? He was here, the morning his mother died, the only one of her eight children to be present...and it was because he was there when his mother died Esme told him a terrible secret.

Memory

"SHE WAS dying. She had been dying for her whole life, and her last pregnancy, my youngest sister, was the one the one that drove the final nail in her coffin. She died because she told my father the truth too late, and his bitter resentment and sense of betrayal made him lose all grasp of reality."

"What betrayal, Mason?" she asked, gripping the bars of his cell, leaning as close as she dared.

"There is a fatal weakness in our line, introduced through my mother. From her mother, a noblewoman in Elysian who married into their royal house. It's a genetic disease, one that has over a 75% chance of being passed from parent to child, regardless of gender. In most it stays dormant, but can become active in the right conditions during childhood illness." Mason's face was free of his usual cynicism. His eyes were as dark as his brothers', and she had no trouble reading hem. He was speaking the truth.

"A weakness? A disease? Tell me! Are my children alright? Do they have it? Does Malcolm?" Panic was seeping into her nerves. Were her babies sick? Her husband. Surely not, they were all so healthy. They must be fine. Her hopes were dashed, and Arianna almost fell off the chair she was using to see into Mason's cell.

"Malcolm has it, sister dear. I have it, and the children have been spared, but they are not spared the fallout from the lies. My sisters, even with the assistance garnered in their births, were born with it. It presents falsely as a form of chicken pox when they're children. My mother, Saints rest her soul, gave the disease to us all, save one."

"What is it?" Arianna whispered, terrified.

"I could go into a horrible, long winded lecture on what it does, but the disease itself has been around for eons, attacking houses that have seen to many inter-marriages of cousins and the like generation after generation. It's a disease that attacks the eggs and sperm cells in developing children, that causes a type of cellular disintegration of the cell walls," Mason said, a weird smile twisting his lips. "There is no treatment for it, not for a Cassian Royal at least."

"I don't understand," Arianna complained, though in part, she did. A deepening well of despair was building in her gut. This couldn't be true.

"The disease, Ari, renders those afflicted with increasing levels of sterility. Most people aren't aware they have it. A fever will occur when a child, growing in severity, then one day be gone as if by magic. But inside the body, especially in females, the cells are becoming weaker. Eggs in the ovaries are becoming warped, breaking down. In advanced cases, like with my mother, the cellular degeneration can spread to the uterus and vaginal walls, even into the intestines. It weakens everything."

"Oh, dear God, no," Ari breathed, in total shock. "My sons? Malcolm?"

"The men luck out, if you want to call it luck. We won't die of it, but Malcolm and I are sterile. It just warps our sperm as its produced, making them weaker, less viable, and eventually we will cease to make any at all."

"But…I have children! They are his! My children are Malcolm's! Stop lying!" Arianna snapped, becoming enraged. This was all a horrible, nasty lie. "I have slept with no man but him!"

"You have children, yes. So does my witch of a wife. They are not sick, but that doesn't matter." Mason smiled, a rueful display of bitterness. "Malcolm is not the father. Nor am I."

"What? What do you mean?"

"King Henry was so upset when my mother started to get sick right after she gave birth to Edward. He was even more upset because my mother miscarried at least twice between Mal and myself, and twice again between me and Edward. Mother wanted to stop having children, you see. She knew what was wrong with her. Why she was having so much trouble getting pregnant and staying that way."

"Tell me who the fathers are!" Arianna shrieked, ready to strangle Mason.

"Once it came time for Malcolm to marry, my father had him tested. Quietly, of course. The disease was in the last stages with Malcolm. He is completely sterile. So am I. But our father couldn't admit this to anyone. The sanctity of the Cassian Dynasty must be preserved above all else, and for him to remove both Mal and I from the line of succession wouldn't do at all. Too much speculation, doubts into the strength of Airric's sons. Our line would be seen as tainted, weakened."

She was going to be sick, he couldn't mean….

"So Father, his blood as pure and untainted as any previous Cassian Monarch, decided that he would guarantee the continuance of our line. He would skip the tainted generation completely. So each year, my dear sister, during your routine visits to the royal physicians, he had you secretly impregnated with another's seed."

"No…" The urge to vomit rose, threatening to overwhelm her.

"Your children are my father's bastards."

Arianna

THE MEMORY left her ill. And so did the slim journal she held in her hand, dated some forty years prior. It was written by the late queen, when she was still Princess Esme of Elysian. Arianna dropped the journal, and dove back into the small chest she'd found under the bed, looking for one that would have been written around the time of her death. Mason was fifteen when his mother died, so Malcolm would have just turned twenty. Arianna married Malcolm the year he turned thirty, just over ten years ago.

Malcolm knew, he must. Mason knew, so therefore Malcolm must know. How could he take her to their marriage bed, make love to her, and celebrate each of her pregnancies knowing the truth? How deeply did this betrayal run?

She found it, a dark blue leather book dated the year of Queen Esme's death. Arianna sat on the floor, skirts askew, and flipped until she found the relevant passages.

The words made her heart pound, her stomach flip. It was true.

King Henry, deprived of a healthy wife and heirs, forced Queen Esme to go through more pregnancies, this time via IVF. His sanity broken, King Henry was determined that he would never let the line of Airric fail, so he felt more children was the answer. It was all done secretly, since no royal could be conceived through artificial means. Only through intercourse and unassisted, natural conception was a Cassian heir considered legitimate. It was written into law almost a hundred years ago, when the development of DNA technologies took off around the world. It was a law created as a measure to insure that only a true-blood Cassian could take the throne, so that no foreign blood could be inserted into the line in an attempt to usurp the crown.

Queen Esme was implanted with an egg fertilized with the king's seed, and forced on bed rest for each pregnancy. Queen Esme was forced to carry each child to term, then they were delivered via C-section. With each reluctant pregnancy and birth, she grew weaker and weaker.

Edward was the last child she conceived and delivered naturally, before the disease began to kill her. All of the blood princesses, while the king's daughters, were automatically disqualified from the line of succession because they were conceived via IVF, and so were all of their children as a result.

Edward, last naturally conceived child, and the only one who wasn't.....

"King Henry will be most upset, sister," a nasty voice interrupted her thoughts, and Arianna sat up sharply, eyes wide in dismay. "You weren't supposed to know."

Camilla stood just inside the door, a smirk on her lips, eyes full of manic delight. She walked into the room, lips twisting in derision. Arianna surged to her feet, enraged.

"You knew! You bitch! You must have known!" Arianna screamed, rounding the bed, intending to rip her sister-in-law to shreds. How dare she take part in this travesty!

"Of course I knew! I've known since Mason was called back from the army to marry me. He refused, the bastard." Camilla's face warped into a snarl, and she dodged Ari's reaching hand. She darted across the room, a small table between them, Arianna panting in rage, bosom heaving. Camilla giggled, some of her insanity slipping out in the sound.

"Why?" She was asking this of everyone. She was so confounded by the whole mess that it was all she could ask past her anger and confusion.

"Why did he refuse? He was in love with a soldier! Because he caught some of Eddie's perversion, that's why," Camilla spat. "Oh? Do you mean why did I go along with this? Easy, sister. I wanted to be a princess."

"For power?" Arianna gasped out, shaking. "You let them violate us for power?"

"Don't act so scandalized. You wed Malcolm for the same reasons. You were never told any of this because you're too flighty, too spoiled. You're dutiful and devoted one moment, and irascible and undependable the next. Too inconstant. Stubborn, even, and King Henry said you weren't to be trusted."

"You let him put his seed in you? You knew what was really happening during our yearly exams?" Arianna demanded, again feeling sick. Her emotions were everywhere, all over the place.

"I let King Henry fuck me," Camilla admitted, and Arianna swayed on her feet. "There was no need to pretend with me, I let him knock me up the good old fashioned way. I've actually never slept with Mason, you know. He could never get it up for me."

"I don't blame him one bit, you disgusting whore!" Arianna lunged for Camilla, but her sister-in-law ran back towards the door, laughing.

"Don't be rude, Ari. King Henry is going to be so mad at you! And Malcolm, well...he's going to be so disappointed you know the truth." Camilla smiled one last time, and then ran out the door.

She would go directly to the King. Of that, Arianna had no doubt. She had little time before she ended up under lock and key, or worse, she ended up like Mason. There was no need for a queen-presumptive, not anymore—there were six heirs for the Crown Prince, after all. Arianna was decoration at this point.

If the king was crazy enough to violate his wife's right to choose, then to do the same to his daughter-in-law's, and everything he'd done to Mason over the years, and now Edward...he was insane enough to kill her.

She would never stay silent. This atrocity could not go unanswered.

There was someone in this palace who could tear this secret apart, and stop King Henry's madness. And there was someone out there now, who's right to rule was pure and unblemished by his father's insanity and duplicity.

CHAPTER FOUR

Percy

"EDWARD?" PERCY called hesitantly, still not used to saying his master's name when other people were around. Reynard was sitting in a chair next to their room's door, long legs stretched out in front of him, gun in his lap, the TV remote in his other, switching through the channels on the unit on mute.

"Yes, Percy?" Edward asked, coming out of the bathroom, drying his hands on a towel.

Percy put a hand on his neck, the consort collar heavier than usual, with the skin underneath becoming irritated. This was the longest stretch of time he'd worn it without Edward removing it to provide his skin with some relief, and he was past the point of being brave and keeping quiet.

Percy tipped his head to the side and lifted the heavy coils, the rope-like collar limp and silky, but the finely refined metal was beginning to hurt him. "It hurts."

Edward walked over the bed where he knelt, Reynard pausing what he was doing to watch. Edward towered over him, his fingers taking the place of Percy's as he lifted the collar higher, exposing the skin on the right side of his neck.

"Damnation," Edward breathed out, gently moving Percy's head so he could see all around his neck. The skin was red and chafed on both sides, the back and front not as irritated. "I am so sorry, Percy. I don't have the key. I lost it after I got shot."

"Let me see," Reynard said, standing at Edward's side now, leaning over Percy's other side. Thick fingers with callused pads ran gently over his skin, and Percy shivered.

"Can you pick it?" Edward asked Reynard, both men touching his neck and the collar. Percy closed his eyes, hyper-aware of the two bigger, stronger men looming over him. Edward meant the ornate locking mechanism that the two ends of the collar disappeared into. It was a dark metal, heavily covered in precious red and white gems, and the ancient collar was designed to fit one key, and one key only, making it nearly impossible for it to be removed by anyone other than the royal who put it on the consort's neck.

"If this was a lock designed in the last fifty years or so, I would say yes," Reynard said, tipping Percy's chin back and lifting the lock away from his neck as high as it could go. "This necklace is over five-hundred years old, and meant to resist tampering. It was created by some of most ingenious and devious men in history. We would need an expert in ancient lock designs. I'll do my best, though."

Percy blinked his eyes open, eyes watering at the sting as the coils dragged on the inflamed flesh of his neck. Reynard froze, and Edward took the necklace from Reynard, holding the coil off of Percy's neck.

"There should be a silk scarf in one of the bags," Edward said to Reynard, who strode for the side of the room where their bags were stacked. Reynard returned after a moment, and handed Edward a long length of silk, and he held a small blue jar in his other hand.

"Put some salve on first, on the skin, then the silk," Reynard advised, opening the small jar. A strong odor rose from it, and Percy crinkled his nose in distaste. Edward chuckled, and dipped his fingers in the creamy ointment.

The second the salve hit his skin, Percy moaned at the cooling sensation, the pain dissipating, going numb. It was cool, and stung, but it quickly went away as Edward spread a thin layer around his neck. Percy leaned into the touch, eyes growing heavy, the care and thoroughness his master showed in tending to him making him want to melt in pleasure. He hummed, and rubbed his jaw and cheek on Edward's forearm, looking up and watching every move his lover made.

Dark eyes met his, and Percy could see a deepening in them, as Edward recognized his fascination and responded. The door clicked somewhere nearby, the captain gone from the room, but Percy couldn't take his eyes off Edward to check. All he wanted was for Edward to keep touching him.

Edward was wiping his hands on a towel now, watching Percy as he kneeled on the bed, biting his lip, shifting his weight. Percy whimpered, his body vibrating with need. Percy reached out and tried to grab Edward, but his master backed away, shaking his head. Percy whined deep in his throat, desperately needing Edward to touch him, to take him, his hole growing wet and aching with emptiness. Percy's body clenched, tight and urgent, and he fell to all fours on the bed, a fine layer of sweat building over his whole body, clothes sticking.

"Edward, I need. Please," he begged, arching his back, spreading his legs apart on the bed. He felt the pull and odd weight of his abdomen, and he groaned, eyes falling shut, his muscles thrumming with need as it radiated out from his core.

He was very aware of his body, how it felt, how empty and yet how full he felt on the inside. His chute clenched and grew slicker, aching deeper, and further in he could feel the firm, almost solid-seeming weight in his womb.

Edward tossed the towel, staring at him. "Take off your clothes, Percy."

He obeyed, scrambling to remove his clothing as fast as he could. He got caught up in his pants and socks, whimpering with frustration. Edward was watching, still as a statue, eyes burning, their dark flames making Percy nearly frantic with need.

Edward

PERCY'S NEED was sudden, even for him. His lovely little mate was always willing, and so highly responsive that Edward took care not to do anything that would excite Percy in public. Yet lately, in the last week or so, Percy's need for sex was explosive.

Percy took off his clothes so fast Edward was sure he tore some seams, and he was kneeling on the bed, his slim, sexy cock hard and throbbing. Pointing up at his bellybutton, Percy's cock was flushed red, his delicious sac pulled in tight, and Edward gestured with his hand, silently asking for Percy to turn around. Percy mewled in need, but obeyed, turning on his knees until Edward could see his pert, firm ass. A look was all he needed to determine that Percy was highly aroused, his natural slick gleaming wet between those luscious cheeks and his rear clenching as his internal muscles prepared for penetration.

Edward went rock hard. So fast his head spun for a second. It didn't matter they were on the run. It didn't matter that Reynard was probably right outside the door, guarding their lives and able to hear everything about to happen in here. All that mattered was getting inside his delectable mate, and fucking him until he screamed Edward's name.

Percy gave a soft, breathy cry, full of ache and need. Edward's cock strained against the zipper of his trousers, and he reached down, unbuttoning them, releasing his shaft and peeling back his boxer briefs. Percy's eyes went to the sight of his freed flesh, and if ice could burn, his glacial blue orbs set Edward on fire. His sexy little mate, skin flushed, breathing ragged, went to his hands, ass high in the air, and all but melted in the mattress. Ass up, shoulders down, Percy presented the most delightful picture, and any restraint Edward had evaporated.

"Saint's blood, Percy," Edward sighed, walking to the bed, hands going to Percy's hips, pulling him to the edge. His hands spanned Percy's lithe waist, leanly muscled and elegantly proportioned. His skin was pure and unblemished, unmarred by the harsh reality of natural and random conception and birth. The slope of his spine, the slight curve of his hips, the sleek muscles on his shoulders, all of Percy was designed with perfection in mind.

Edward worshipped that perfection. Eyes tracing over every inch of Percy he could see, his hands following in the path of his gaze, skin humming with desire, Edward beat back his baser instincts, remembering that while Percy was built for sex, and relished in the rougher side of things, his beautiful mate was bearing his child. No matter how badly he wanted to mount and rut away mindlessly, he would cherish and protect his mate and babe.

"Please, Edward," Percy begged him, voice quiet, soft, his hips lifting to push into his hands. "I need you."

"Settle," Edward instructed him, holding Percy still. Edward lowered his trousers and underwear out of the way, and stepped closer. He guided his cock to Percy's slicked crease, rubbing the flared head in the musky and sweet fluid, both of their breathing patterns hitching in reaction as he pressed to Percy's willing hole. "Do you want me inside you, my mate?"

"Yee-s-s-ss," Percy tried to say, fingers digging into the blankets, and Edward held him still when he attempted to push back and impale himself on Edward's cock.

"Anything for you," Edward promised, and pushed in. Percy gave a small, aborted cry, his breath failing as Edward sank to the hilt.

So tight, hot, wet, with powerful muscles immediately milking his organ. Edward moaned, adjusting Percy's hips, finding the perfect angle, and withdrawing just enough to push back inside with some force behind his thrust. His mate gave him a tiny sound, full of want and overcome nerves. Fire ran along his body, from where his cock was buried in perfection and up his spine, setting fire to his thoughts.

Hard, short thrust in, head nudging at the place their child grew, and a slow, ever so slow withdrawal, delighting in the slick, smooth flesh of Percy's channel. Edward's eyes closed, and his world narrowed to the flesh welcoming his cock and the vibrating body under his hands. He rotated his hips, adding depth to his thrusts, and Percy sobbed each time he did it.

Edward became lost in the feel and sounds of Percy, so welcoming, so fucking sexy. He repeated his pattern, eyes closed, totally focused on his mate coming apart under his hands. He let go of worry and stress, anger and fear, and gave himself to Percy's pleasure, finding satisfaction as Percy quivered and whimpered.

"So perfect," Edward told the shaking bundle of desire crying his name as he continued his devastating pattern, each stroke in damn near catching him in an unshakeable grip of powerful muscles. Percy was close, his body tightening on Edward, every stroke bringing them both closer to climax and release.

"Edward!" Percy shrieked, his whole body bowing as an orgasm slammed into his small mate. Edward thrust home, opening his eyes to watch as Percy's body sucked him impossibly deeper.

His body was humming. Every nerve swamped in heat and undulating waves of pleasure. Edward came as Percy's body clamped down on his cock, and Edward poured everything he had into the heated depths, his seed all but sucked out of him. Balls tight and aching, Edward stopped breathing, whole body incapable of moving, his cock and balls pulsing in time together, his body's focus locked into the sinful grip of Percy's.

Edward

HE MUST have blacked out. Lack of oxygen causing him to fall to the bed, Percy trapped under his greater weight, his little mate still milking his cock in lessening waves. Percy was asleep, and Edward eased from his seed-slicked chute, grabbing his mate around the waist and pulling Percy into his arms.

Percy slept on, totally relaxed. Edward ran his fingers over the back of his slim neck, the raw flesh from the consort collar worse along the sides where the slight slack in the coils rubbed as Percy moved. Edward sat up with care, and searched on the bed for the silk scarf, finding it down among their feet. Percy was so deeply asleep Edward was able to wrap the consort collar in the fine silk, covering the coils all the way around, running out of fabric near the jewel-encrusted lock.

Edward used the tassels at each end to secure the silk, and he dropped his hands away with one last brush to Percy's skin, smooth as the silk that now protected him from further damage.

The consort necklace was ancient, and Edward had lost count of how many consorts in times past had worn the same collar. One collar, one key, both created at the same time, both equally priceless. And the collar had been designed as both protection for the one collared, and a mark of ownership. Only a Cassian Royal, most commonly the princes of the blood, had the right to collar a consort, and as such each lock had been created unique, by individual masters, and there was no way to remove it without either damaging the relic or damaging the one who wore it.

Not all consorts in the old days had been willing.

Many collars in ancient times had come booby-trapped,

small vials of acid concealed inside the clasps, rigged to break if the lock was forced. Those were used on royal prisoners of war, or those who were especially recalcitrant in their new roles as slaves. No rescue of a captured foreign royal could be successful if the removal of the consort collar left the wearer dead. After one horrible, tragic attempt three hundred years ago, no one had ever tried again.

Edward had chosen a collar with a less nefarious history, commissioned by a Crown Prince five hundred years ago for his lover, a young princess captured on her travels along Cassia's borders. The tale went that she was on her way to be wed to another, and the Crown Prince had seen her beauty and coveted her for his own, ambushing her caravan at a small border town with Elysian. He took her as consort, fathering the next generation of royals off her, and she eventually became Queen-Consort when he took the throne. Whether one believed the historical version of a spoiled prince stealing and forcing an innocent maiden into sexual slavery or the love tale from folklore was up to the mindset of the current master. Edward chose to believe in the tale of love and passion instead of villainy and rape. Its history came with more love than tragedy attached to its storied past.

The key, usually on a slim necklace of its own, had hung around Edward's neck since the day he collared his young mate. It was lost somewhere between getting shot in the square and escaping the hospital the next day. Edward needed to find someone to remove the necklace, or they needed to get their hands on the tools to do it themselves. If they went to someone else to remove it they ran the risk of being recognized and reported; Edward had no idea what kind of tool could safely remove the coils from Percy's neck without injury to his mate, since bolt cutters wouldn't do—the metal was too dense, too resistant to cutting. Crafted from the rarest of metals, each collar was built to withstand all serious attempts at removal.

Perhaps the easiest means to remove it would be to pick the lock. Surely today's techniques could outwit the ancient lockmasters of old.

CHAPTER FIVE

Percy

PERCY PACED, the twelve steps it took to walk from one side of the room to the other too short to occupy his mind. Edward was speaking to Reynard in the hall, their voices muffled by the door. Percy huffed, and glared at the door, pausing a moment. Nothing happened, and he began pacing again. He was frustrated, and tired, and all he wanted was for Edward to hold him, to pull him close and tell him everything was going to be fine.

The collar about his neck was wrapped in silk, and while it provided his skin relief from the constant rubbing of the coils, it made him hot. He was sweating, and his back hurt, and he was about to climb the walls if he didn't some relief!

Percy stopped pacing, tired, and arched his back, trying to soothe the dull ache at the base of his spine. He stretched, and he gasped as a muscle in his abdomen pulled. His baby bump was bigger.

Noticeably bigger.

His clothing wasn't fitting, his trousers had to be unbuttoned at the waist, and all of the expensive fabric irritated his skin. He was most comfortable in Edward's sweatpants and shirtless, but he couldn't wear that all the time. Finding an inn willing to clean their clothes was hard, since all their clothes were Prince Mason's, and required specialty cleaning. Reynard has been buying them new clothes as they traveled, but they had a finite amount of money and Reynard had cautioned Edward that they had to be careful with what they had left.

"My prince..." the volume increased on the other side of the door, and Percy shot it an irritated glance. Reynard spent his time cautioning Edward to stay out of sight, but then he would constantly call Edward by his title. Even Percy knew that servants were everywhere and overheard everything, and this was a small inn.

Whatever was going on out there in the hallway wasn't good. Reynard had returned not long after Percy fell asleep in Edward's arms, and despite his ironclad control, Percy could see the captain was rattled. Edward wasted no time in grabbing his arm and taking Reynard back out into the shadowed hall, closing the door behind them. Time was dragging on for Percy and he was ready to just....

Percy stomped to the door. As he got closer, he could hear the strained tones of his lover and the captain, all but hissing at each other. He couldn't hear any words clearly enough through the door, and he was so tired of everything. Percy grabbed the door and flung it open so hard a draft kicked up. Reynard and Edward both jumped, staring at him.

"Edward. Reynard," Percy said, breathing hard. "You're in the hallway. Talking. Where I can't hear. I'm tired, and hot, and my back hurts, and ***you can stop hiding things from me!***"

He wailed that last part, the incredulity on their faces enough to remind Percy that he never, not once in all his life, ever acted out. He'd been in a cage his whole life, and now he was out in the world and the most horrible thing was that he might have been safer in the cage because then he knew who was going to hurt him **and... and... and... and**......he was sobbing.

Percy backed away from the door, leaving it open wide, and he hugged himself, sobs wracking his body in horrible jerks. He clutched at his shoulders, but that was too hot, and then he dropped them, but then he was too cold, and he hit his baby bump by accident and then.....Percy stood alone in the middle of the bedroom and cried.

"Little one?" came a hesitant inquiry, Edward cautiously approaching him, hand outstretched.

Percy turned away, wiping at his tears. He was so tired of crying. What was wrong with him? Percy didn't want to be crying anymore. He was helpless and he didn't know anything, and Edward and Reynard had to explain the simplest things to him......

"Shh, little one," Edward soothed, his more than capable hands gently pulling him closer. Percy collapsed on his chest, crying into Edward's shirt. His tears wouldn't stop. Why wouldn't they stop?

"What's...what's wrong ...with me?" Percy tried to speak, words interrupted by sobs. Eyes scrunched up, nose pressed to the firm swell of muscle over his lover's heart, Percy was falling apart.

"Nothing, my love," Edward whispered in his ear. "You're pregnant, and instead of being safe and secure at home in Hartgrove, we're in a strange town in a strange place. There is nothing wrong with you, but the world. So cry until you can't cry anymore, and I'll talk you through our options."

"Don't wanna...don't wanna cry..."

"There is nothing wrong with your tears," Edward replied, stern and tender. "Anyone who complains about your tears will receive a reason to cry themselves."

"Can't make everyone cry," Percy sniffled.

"Watch me," Edward whispered to him, and Percy giggled. He smiled, the tears leaving as fast as they came, and Percy hugged Edward back. He leaned on his lover, and Edward let him, his embrace welcoming and steadfast.

Percy opened his eyes, and he accepted the handkerchief Reynard held out to him. He wiped his face, and Reynard gripped the nape of his neck with a big, callused hand, squeezing once before dropping away.

He was worn out, but strangely enough his mind was alert. He pressed his cheek to Edward's chest, arms about his waist, and let Edward rock them side to side gently. Percy pushed closer, his baby bump against Edward's thigh, and a big hand fell to caress him.

"Better?"

"Yes. I'm sorry," Percy whispered.

"You did nothing wrong, little one," Edward assured him. "Come sit on the bed with me, and Reynard and I will tell you what's going on."

Edward sat with him on the bed, Percy in his lap, his master's hand still on his belly, rubbing the taut flesh. Edward's touch felt so good, and Percy melted into his arms. Reynard went to a chair across from them, long legs out and crossed at the ankles. His jacket gaped, and Percy saw a gun snug in a holster under his left arm. Dark jacket, dark shirt, dark pants, Reynard was a shadow, but for his rich auburn hair and twilight blue eyes, offset by pale skin and a stony expression.

Reynard was tense. Even appearing relaxed, slouched in the chair, hands over his stomach, there was a tension that hovered about the captain.

"What's wrong?" Percy asked, oddly relaxed. The words came easily, far easier than they would have even a week ago.

"There are royal guards in town. The barracks just on the outskirts of town is active, and ten royal guards arrived about an hour ago," Edward said, rubbing Percy's belly.

"Are they…do they know we're here?" Percy asked.

"If they knew for certain we were here, they'd have us already," Reynard replied. "They must be responding to a tip or a reported sighting. If not for us, then perhaps for the local… nobleman. This is the closest I've seen the guards in days."

"Can we get out of town?" Percy said, as Edward caressed him, hand dipping dangerously low as his lover swept the whole of the bump. Edward was trying to feel the baby, but the tiny one was always sleeping, rarely moving when Edward tried to feel for him or her.

"Maybe," Reynard said. "This is a small town, and the Estiary estate surrounds it on three sides. Only way out back to the highway is past the barracks."

Reynard's face gave a small twitch as he said the name, and Edward paused in his motions, hand stilling before he continued on.

"Estiary," Percy stated. Reynard's eyes flicked to him, lightning swift, before going to Edward. "Why do you both react like that?"

"Lord Lucius Meriele, sixth Baron of Estiary, is the local lord and the one who owns most of the land in this area." Edward stopped rubbing him, arms coming up to cradle him close. "Lord Estiary is also one of the most prolific buyers of pleasure slaves in the country. His harem is almost mythical for its slaves."

Percy's body went cold. He pulled his feet in, and curled up as small as he could, Edward gathering him close. "Breeders?"

"Only a few, just enough to get heirs," Edward said, "but he has a penchant for perfection, and his harem is rumored to only hold the most beautiful slaves ever created. He is most jealous of them, and will go out his way to procure the best as the breeding houses make them."

"He was also banished from court about ten years ago, around the time Prince Malcolm and Princess Arianna wed," Reynard said, and Percy was barely able to hear him past the rushing of blood in his ears. "Lord Estiary was banned from setting foot in the capital for crimes against the crown. Unspecified, but King Henry, for whatever reason, didn't have him arrested. Whatever his offenses, it's been speculated he has something holding off the King, so his punishment was banishment instead of prison."

Percy shut down. He could care less about whatever Lord Estiary and the king had between them. His courage failed him at the thought of breeding houses. The place of his birth, for all that it was predictable and familiar, was now a place of horror. He knew what life was meant to be, in some way at least, and living in a cage was not life. And if Heritage ever got their hands on Percy, he would lose his babe, lose Edward, and spend his life in a dark cell, raped and bred and cloned.

"We need to go. I say we wait until early morning, then drive out," Reynard offered. "We stay here any longer and someone is going to say something. You're too recognizable, my prince, and if Estiary catches wind that there's a collared slave in town, he will know immediately who it is. Percy's the only collared breeder in the whole world. Whether Estiary would alert the crown is a hit and miss, but I don't want to risk it."

"Agreed. We get some rest now, then we leave at dawn," Edward said, and Percy was glad. They needed to leave. Hopefully the guards weren't here for them, and this was just happenstance that they were here, so far from Hartgrove and where they should be looking.

Why were the guards here? Did someone see them, report them to the palace? Maybe they had nothing to worry about, and the guards were merely here to check that Lord Estiary was obeying the banishment order.

Were the guards even here for them?

Mason - Several days ago

BLOOD ALMOST made him lose his grip.

Mason flipped his wrist, and the guard's arm snapped. He fell, screaming to the floor, but Mason's knee to the back of the head silenced him. Mason jumped over the guard, grabbing the metal tray that held his paltry dinner of stale bread and grayish gravy, and swung it across the face of the next man through the door. A resounding clang and the crumpled mess of limbs told him the man was out, and Mason stepped out of his cell, pulling the door shut behind him.

Arianna gaped at him, mouth open, eyes wide. A handful of keys, a cell phone, and a dark leather jacket hung from her hands, and Mason grabbed them before she could drop them from her senseless fingers. She'd made excellent time. A part of him was certain she would have been caught running back and forth between his cell and room, but she'd made it back in time for his dinner tray. His father must be looking for her, given Camilla's interference. If he wasn't, then sometime soon he would be.

"Don't worry, dear sister," Mason quipped, pulling the jacket on, and pocketing the keys. He woke the cell, and made sure it was one he could use before pocketing it. It was from the hidden stash in his room, and the battery was full. "I don't think I killed them. I'm not too sure, though. Blood loss may have impaired my control. You can check if you like."

Mason strode past her, glad his boots weren't thrown away, since the stones of the Old Palace were ice cold. He heard the patter of slippered feet behind him, and Arianna followed him, her skirts rustling over the stones. He waited, and sure enough, she found her voice after a few turns deeper into the Old Palace.

"Mason…" He spun, putting his hand over her mouth. She stopped, and then her eyes narrowed in a glare and she yanked her head away.

"Shush," Mason said, pointing at her face, which made her glare even more. His sister-in-law looked ready to kill, and he smiled. "No talking."

He walked down the unlit corridor, heading for the throne room, buried in the center of Airric's castle. He counted, and after about 30 seconds, Arianna's control wavered.

"Why are we going to the old throne room? Aren't you supposed to be escaping?"

Mason kept walking, listening for echoes of pursuit. Anyone chasing him now would likely think as Arianna did, and that he would try and get out of the palace. He would, but not just yet. He needed something first, and there was always a way out of the palace for a royal son.

After a few minutes, Mason paused outside the heavy doors of the throne room. He listened, but at this time of night, there was no one about. He opened the ancient portals, slipping inside, Arianna clutching his elbow as he led the way into the shadowed cavernous throne room. She had likely never been here in years, probably not since the grand tour of the palace before she wed Malcolm a decade earlier.

The long room was cast in darkness, and he decided against the lanterns. There was just enough light in the throne room to illuminate the way. Airric's throne, as ancient as the castle in which it sat, rose high from the low dais. Mason walked faster. To be this close, only to be caught, would be the height of cruelty, and considering fate's treatment of him the last twenty years, he figured he had better hurry.

Arianna was all but running to keep up. He jumped onto the dais, and went to the side of the throne. The ancient wood was polished by the centuries, heavy, battle-scared, bearing the marks of betrayal and attempted coups. In ancient times, the throne had been modified to hide weapons inside it, so that the king or queen upon the throne would have a last line of defense. One long-ago queen had even placed a small crossbow equipped with poisoned bolts in the throne. The line of Airric lay unbroken due to that precaution.

It was no crossbow he was after. He found the latch, small and hidden inside a burl near the base. Pressing it, the base of the throne gave a small sigh of sound, and slid to the side.

"What is that?" Arianna hissed in a bad approximation of a whisper. She really was bad at subterfuge.

"A secret. No peeking," Mason said, and she kicked at his ass with a dainty slipper. "Dammit, woman! I've been tortured for days, and your first impulse is to kick me?"

"I'll do more than that if you don't start telling me what you're doing! We're going to be caught!"

Mason ignored her, which earned him another tap on the ass, but he reached down and into the small void at the throne's base. His fingers found what he needed, and he pulled out a dark object, hiding it from Ari's sight. It went under his jacket, and he reached back in.

Deeper than before, he found the stone lever, and yanked.

Nothing happened at first. Quiet ruled the ancient room, and the dust swirled in the faint light. Arianna huffed behind him, and Mason listened.

A hollow groan reverberated through the room, the floor vibrating. Echoes bounced off the walls, and Arianna gasped, spinning, trying to see the cause of the noise.

Mason smiled. He carefully put the hidden panel back in place, and stood. His body was sore, and tired, but he was damned if he was going to spend one more fucking night in this wretched prison.

The palace stopped being home the day his mother revealed the truth, letting him read her journals as her life bled out through internal injuries that could never be repaired, the disease destroying her body from the inside out. She died, his father watching unseen from the door, Mason crying at her bedside, clutching her forgotten journal in his hands. Mason had thrown himself at his father in righteous anger, only to be knocked to the floor, mouth bleeding.

That moment was the exact time the palace stopped being home, and his father became someone to hate.

"Ari," Mason said. She turned from her search, and waited. "I still think you're a spoiled brat. You care more for fashion and Malcolm's crown than you do anything else, but I've never meant you harm. I'm sorry I didn't tell you sooner."

"I love my children." Arianna replied softly. She walked forward, and hugged him, surprising him. He hugged her back for a brief moment before backing away. She gave him a bitter smile. "I love them enough to be angry at their real father, but never angry enough to regret them. You need to leave, Mason. My children need me to stay."

"He might kill you."

"He might," Arianna said, stepping back, taking the high step back down the main floor of the throne room, backing away. "Then if this is the last time I'm ever going to see you, I should tell you that I don't really dislike you all that much. I have a suspicion that your escape had something to do with that noise, so I'm going to leave before I see exactly how you get out. That way I won't be lying when I tell them I don't know anything."

"Smarter than you look," he murmured, backing away into the shadows. "Be careful, Arianna."

He turned away, and headed for the heavily shadowed doorway in the wall behind the throne. There lay King Airric's old bedroom, and inside, the ancient escape route he found as child. The knowledge was lost to the centuries, and Mason was certain that no one other than he recalled that there was a tunnel under the Old Castle, leading out past the new palace's boundaries. Not even his brothers knew.

"End this madness, Mason," she called after him, voice fading as the distance between them grew. "Cleanse the line of Airric of his insanity."

Mason found the secret door beneath Airric's ancient bed. Thankful he stayed in shape after leaving the army, he slithered under the bed and let himself fall through the hole in the floor. He landed hard, and lay gasping on the dusty floor of the tunnel for a moment before picking himself up. He stood, and hit the lever next to the trap door. The door slowly lifted back into place, dropping him in total darkness.

He rested there in the dark, categorizing his injuries, how his body felt. While it was painful moving, and the contusions and burns across his torso hurt like blazes, he'd had worse. Years of being beaten and tortured while on missions for the Crown left him with a higher tolerance for pain and misery, and he was thankful for it now. Even years later, his father's worst barely matched the least of his ordeals in the military. Though he was older now, and he hadn't been tortured in a good long while. Physically at least, his marriage to Camilla was horrific on a daily basis. Traveling would still be a bitch, but pain was nothing against the chance for vengeance. He would push himself until he either failed or flourished.

Mason put a hand to the wall, his eyes useless. He would save the cell's flashlight app for when the tunnel began to branch out, but for the next several hundred feet it was straight as an arrow. He walked, unafraid, hand flat to the rough stone wall.

The air was stale, dusty. Smelled of earth and old things. All would be worrisome to others, but it reassured him. No one had been in this passage in years. The secret was still safe.

Mason put a hand to his chest, the object he took from Airric's throne safe in his pocket. He had a plan.

Get out of the palace in one piece. Sort of, but close enough.

Get out of the city without being captured. Problematic, but doable.

Find the equipment he needed to start burning down his father's walls of deceit. About damn time.

Find Reynard and his charges. Mason would avoid looking towards Hartgrove and the northern mountains. The king and his ministers were cold men, unaware of common things like compassion and real love, so they would look where they would go, and not where decent men would. Hartgrove was were Edward went to feel safe, his place of power, and so Hartgrove was being watched for just that reason.

Edward and Reynard would take Percy not to a place where they could keep him out of harm's way and locked away from the world.

No.

Edward loved Percy, and would want what was best for Percy, and not himself. That meant they would head east. Towards Elysian and freedom. Mason would find them in that direction.

He walked on, the dark comforting. More time to think and plan.

CHAPTER SIX

Percy

DAWN WAS arriving, illuminating the forest. The SUV sat idling, the engine noise barely a ripple of disturbance in the mist and dampened quiet. Gold light seeped through the pines, and Percy huddled in the back on the vehicle, watching over the back of the seats as the guard barracks was revealed by the fleeing mist. Two vehicles, similar to the one he sat in, were parked outside the building, and there was no sign of movement. It was a small building, and never manned all the time from Reynard's description. It was used as a place for patrols to stop on the way to somewhere else.

The main road out of the small town went directly by the barracks, and traffic was light, but steadily increasing. Their vehicle wouldn't be the only one on the road, and Percy relaxed, waiting for Reynard to put it in gear and get them out of there.

Edward sat in the passenger seat in the front, a gun in his lap. While Edward assured him he knew how to shoot, Percy could see the stress that Edward was under just holding the weapon. He was very aware of it, as if afraid it might come alive at any moment and do something horrible.

Reynard was flipping through radio channels, static alternating between garish beats and wailing that made Percy's ears itch in complaint. He wasn't particularly interested in anything, merely using it as a means to pass the time. He stopped it when he got to something Edward told Percy was a news channel.

"...the video uploaded to the internet three days ago has been confirmed by independent specialists as Prince Mason. The blood prince is shown to be extensively injured, perhaps even tortured as he ascertains in the video. The short clip, only thirty seconds long, shows the second born blood prince sitting in a dark room, covered in bandages, and claiming to have been tortured by King Henry…"

Percy froze. The radio went to commercial break. Reynard's hand, hovering over the dial, shook with a hard tremor. Edward went still, body tense, staring at the radio as an ad for beer played.

Reynard moved. In a flash he was out of the SUV, the door open, and running down the road. The sun was rising, chasing the mist, and he would alternately disappear then reappear as he ran. Edward cursed, and made to follow, but he recalled himself and sat still, though the gun was in his hand and the safety clicked off ominously. He slid out of his seat and into the driver's, closing the door.

Percy crawled over the seat, and up to the front of the vehicle. He took Edward's old seat, and tried to see the captain.

Reynard was at the barracks, slinking low as he ran far swifter than anyone should be able to at a half-crouch. Reynard blended in the rapidly shifting shadows, dawn's light touching the top of the building, and creeping lower. The windows of the barracks were dark, no movement inside, and Percy held his breath, afraid to take his eyes off Reynard for even a second.

The captain, kneeling now at the rear latch of one of the vehicles, did something, and the door opened. Reynard disappeared into the big vehicle, and Percy was at ten seconds when Reynard slithered back out, closing the door with extreme care. He had a medium sized black bag over his shoulder, and he ran through the remaining mist to the other side of the road. Percy was just about to ask why he wasn't running back to their vehicle when the front door of the barracks opened, and a man stepped out.

Edward put the SUV in gear, and they began driving. The guard had his hands up at his face, and Percy sighed in relief when he saw a white plume of smoke come out from behind his hands. The guard continued smoking as Edward drove by, staying at the speed limit. The guard didn't even spare them more than a casual glance as they passed.

Percy tried to see Reynard in the trees as they went by the place he disappeared into, but he could see nothing past the mist and shadows. Edward drove on, and Percy turned in his seat, worried.

"Edward? What about Reynard?"

"Please, little one," Edward said, tense and abrupt. Percy sat back, clicking on his seat belt.

Edward was mad. Very mad.

They drove for a few minutes, going slow, until they rounded a curve in the road. A shadow stepped out in front of them, and Percy squeaked in alarm. Edward stopped the SUV, and Reynard walked around the front to the rear passenger door. Edward let him in, and Percy turned in his seat, gaping at the captain.

He must have ran through the woods to meet them, and he wasn't even breathing hard. He put the bag on the seat next to him, and Edward began driving again. Reynard pulled out a laptop and a small square device. He turned them on, tiny beeps and the even hum of electronics was the only sound for a few minutes.

"Wait a moment, my prince," Reynard said when Edward paused at an intersection, the signs for the royal highway pointing the way. "I'm almost....I got it."

"What?" Percy asked, peering around the seatback. Reynard flipped the laptop around, the screen showing a video paused. Edward checked the road behind them, put the SUV in park, and turned as well. His face and jaw were tight, his dark eyes furious, but Edward held his tongue.

Reynard hit play. Percy gasped, hand over his mouth.

"I won't bother introducing myself. On the night of fireworks celebration, my little brother was almost killed by a stable master in the employ of Heritage Breeders. Those men were under the protection of my father, the king, who were attempting to steal Edward's beloved consort Percy and return him to Heritage. There was no random assassination attempt. Percy is pregnant with Edward's child, and my brother loves him. Percy is in danger. Edward is in danger. Not from unseen foes, but from family. Our family."

Mason leaned forward, face inches from the camera. Dark eyes so like Edward's were full of anger, and what Percy could only guess was betrayal. "King Henry is insane. He spent the last week torturing me because I helped my little brother escape. Don't stop running, Edward. There is madness in the line of Airric, and it festers in our father."

The video cut out. Percy stared, overcome by disbelief.

"It's all over the internet, my prince," Reynard whispered, gripping the screen. "Once one video is pulled down, it goes back up again. It's been shared over ten thousand times already, and growing."

"Saint's blood, what is he doing?" Edward breathed, slumping in his seat, dark eyes shocked.

"I think we need to ask him," Reynard said.

"How do we do that?" Percy whispered, at a loss.

Reynard pulled the laptop back around, and went tapping away on the keyboard. He paused, then turned the screen back around. He pointed, at what looked to be reports of some kind. Percy tried understanding it, but the acronyms and times were confusing, and he shook his head at Reynard, lost.

"Fuck," Edward growled through clenched teeth, and he punched the steering wheel.

"The guards have been attempting to track Mason. They aren't looking for us right now at all. Apparently the king is trying to patch up the damage Mason is causing. They can track the videos to the places they've been uploaded from, but not until hours after it's been uploaded and Mason has moved on. Mason has two more videos, all time stamped a day apart. The one I played was the first one."

"Hold on, you said they were tracking Mason. He's around here?" Edward asked suddenly.

"Last video was uploaded less than a hundred miles from here, around noon yesterday. The guards are attempting to find him. The whole area is flooded with guard squadrons."

"Dammit! What is he doing?"

"Trying to save us all, I think," Reynard said, leaning back in the seat. "There are secrets he has carried for years, and I think he's finally in a place where he can let the lies go."

"While bringing down the weight of my father's wrath at the same time! We were in the clear! Those reports said they have no idea where the three of us are, but now Mason is dragging them after us!"

"No. They narrowed down the search area to a hundred miles. The guards are at the barracks here only because there is a station for them to stop for the night. They are heading out soon, back to the search grid. Mason won't be anywhere near where he was when he uploaded it."

"I'm getting us off the road," Edward said, throwing the SUV into gear and driving. Trees went by in a blur for several minutes, and then he made a hard turn. Edward took them off the paved road, down a narrow dirt road surrounded by a wall of trees on all sides, until they were out of sight of the main road.

Edward threw the SUV into park and killed the engine. Dust billowed up around the SUV, covering the windshield, and Edward got out of the vehicle. Edward shouted, a wordless scream of anger and frustration. He kicked the side of the vehicle, and then fell to his shoulder on it, clutching at his leg. Percy climbed out of the SUV, and went to Edward.

"Your leg?" Percy asked, small hands going to the recovering wound. Edward moved his away, shifting so his back was to the vehicle, and Percy checked for bleeding. Edward rubbed his face, hard, breathing ragged as he tried to calm himself.

Reynard stayed in the SUV. Percy was thankful. Edward needed space. His lover was teetering on the edge again. Reynard's precipitous actions in acquiring the hardware at the barracks, and now Mason's unexplained move against the crown was almost too much for Edward. His master was so used to having everything go smoothly, as he decreed, and always, always being in charge.

Edward wasn't bleeding. Though he probably hurt himself kicking the car like that. Percy leaned on the vehicle at his side, not touching. Just waiting. Letting him calm down, regain his control.

Minutes passed. The woods around them came alive, a few brave birds singing. It was very late winter, nearly spring. The pines were a deep green, the bare maples and birch trees thin and wisplike in the breeze.

Percy sighed, finding the wind was calm, almost warm, and he put his hands on his belly, enjoying the peace. He listened to the woods, and he smiled when he felt a flutter under his palms. Percy reached out, and took Edward's hand. He put it on his stomach, and he could feel when Edward sensed the same thing he did.

Their babe moved, waking up. Tiny pulses of movement, little twitches, but strong. Edward sucked in a deep breath, his whole body stilling. He pushed, so gentle, and Percy smiled with a laugh as their baby moved again, stronger—as if saying hello. Edward jumped, a surprised laugh coming from his lips as well. Percy found himself in a tight embrace, Edward rocking them both on their feet, his face peppered with kisses from his mate.

"I love you," Edward gasped out between kisses, making Percy giggle again.

"I love you too, Edward."

Percy cuddled into Edward, pressing his face to Edward's

neck, breathing him in, Edward's face to his hair. They stood like that, their child moving in small leaps between them.

"Damn them all," Edward said, exasperated more than angry. His lover's anger was washing away, and Percy kissed his neck, happy to see him leaving it behind.

Edward tipped his head back, finger on his chin. Percy smiled, and Edward kissed him, a sweet press of lips. Percy leaned into him, wanting more, but the world was waiting.

Edward pulled back, and led him to the open door of the SUV. Percy clambered in, sitting in the front seat, while Edward got back in and closed the door. Percy gave Reynard a smile, curling up on the cushion, waiting for Edward to decide what they were going to do.

Reynard watched Edward. The captain gave nothing away, expression closed off, but Percy could see a glimmer of something in his dark blue eyes. Worry, perhaps. This was the biggest emotional outburst from Edward that either of them had seen, and Reynard must be at something of a loss.

Edward looked at Reynard in the rearview mirror. "Where is my brother?"

"I can make a very good guess, my prince," Reynard offered without hesitation.

"Tell me," Edward said, simple, to the point.

"Lord Estiary's estate."

Reynard

THERE WAS very little doubt that Prince Edward thought him insane. The glare the prince gave him was vicious, but Abe held his ground. There was no doubt in his mind that Mason was nearby. He was uploading videos to the internet, each one a damning disclaimer of the Cassian Dynasty, and the general trail Mason was leaving behind for the guards to follow was within driving distance.

"Lord Estiary owns the internet relays, the cell tower, the electrical hub and the towers used for satellite communications in this part of the country. Everything sent and received electronically in a hundred mile radius goes through Estiary's estate, my prince. Because of all of the equipment, Estiary has military level firewalls and hardware with software it would take the Crown a year just to break. The man may be a deviant," Abe said, meaning Estiary's fondness for owning pleasure slaves, "But he is a rich son of a bitch who'd delight in keeping King Henry at arm's length. If Mason is going to be anywhere, he'll be there."

"You know my brother that well?" Edward asked, dark eyes intent.

"I do," Reynard replied, holding his prince's gaze, trying to impart just how sure he was.

"Do you believe Estiary is helping him?"

"I say it's a good chance. Lucius hates the king. Mason is obviously trying to burn down the royal house. Get me close enough, I can reconnoiter, see if Mason is there, that way we don't risk Estiary seeing Percy before we know whose side he's on."

"Would he....is he dangerous?" Percy asked, pretty blue eyes wide, curled up like a kitten on the seat. Abe resisted the urge to pull him in for a hug, Edward watching him.

Abe looked at Edward, waiting for him to tell Percy no, that Estiary wouldn't want him the second he laid eyes on the perfection that was Perseus, royal consort. Yet Edward made it a point to never lie to Percy, and this time was no exception. His thoughts mirrored the prince's.

"He covets perfection, my love. You would be the sublime representation of it in Estiary's eyes."

"Is that bad?" Percy whispered, hugging his knees as best he could around the baby bump that was getting more prevalent with each passing day.

"Your looks are not your fault, nor are the reactions others have or will have to them, Perseus," Abe said firmly, refusing to let Percy feel he was to blame for anything. "A man's actions are always his own, even when faced with no options."

Percy nodded, biting his lip, and he curled up even tighter.

"Up to you, my prince," Abe told Edward. "We can continue on to the border. It's still over a thousand miles away. Percy will be safe there, but we still need to actually get to Elysian. Or we can find Mason, and you can ask him what secrets he's been carrying that would warrant your father destroying his whole life."

Edward faced front, eyes to the woods. Abe watched his profile, the prince thinking hard. Abe waited, though his heart was screaming at him to pressure Edward into choosing finding Mason. Mason was a formidable fighter, and while Percy would be safer over the border in Elysian, getting there would be problematic. Every day they risked being recognized, and the royal guards would hear of it, especially once it hit the internet. And it would, too. A royal sighting was an almost instant viral hit. Even out here in the wilds of the greenwoods people had cellphones.

It was a miracle from the Saints that they hadn't been recognized yet.

"Percy?" Edward turned to his mate, tone questing for input. Percy gulped, but he looked Edward in the eye and chose.

"I want to help Mason. We owe him everything."

Edward nodded. He looked back at Abe, dark eyes bright. "Tell me where I'm driving."

Reynard

HE STOOD in the shade of a wind-worn pine, eyes trained on the relay station sitting on a knoll about two hundred meters inside Lord Estiary's estate. It was noon, the winter sun pale, but warmer than it was even a week ago. Spring was coming, still a far off prospect, but coming none the less.

The relay station was huge, three towers rising a hundred feet in the air behind a twenty foot chain link fence capped by razor-wire. Concrete bunkers rested at the feet of the towers, holding the fiber optics, the electrical, satellite and numerous other vital communications systems hardware and wiring for the entire region. Only a fool would think that Lord Estiary wasn't aware of every single word that was spoken or typed, since every mode of communication came through his property. Abe had a feeling that it was that level of control and access to information that Estiary possessed which both earned him the king's wrath and protected him from it. Estiary was too dangerous to keep in the capital, and too dangerous to dispose of—so he was banished. Having only met the man in passing in his youth, Abe had no personal opinion of Lord Estiary, other than one of caution.

Abe watched. It was an unmanned station. There should be no activity unless it was scheduled maintenance, and there was a single one lane dirt road weaving through the trees that accessed the station.

So there shouldn't be a black motorcycle resting on its kickstand just inside the fence, the section cleanly cut and peeled back. The bike was unfamiliar, but the style of its design, and the black helmet hanging from the handles, spoke of a certain personality. Abe felt a spark of hope in his chest.

Away from king and capital, would Mason be willing to let his forced vows fall to the side? They were both out of reach of king and false duty, so maybe there was a chance….that they could be more than stolen moments and clandestine meetings.

Abe knew it was that wish that let the man sneak up on him—his attention taken in by youthful dreams of love and romance. He felt like a fool when the cold snap of a safety being clicked off sounded behind him.

Abe froze, mentally cursing his inattention, and he slowly lifted his hands, palms empty. He turned, making no sudden movements, and met the eyes of the gunman.

"For Saint's sake, Abe, even Percy would've gotten the drop on you," Mason snarked, one brow raised as he lowered the weapon and holstered it. "Miss me?"

"You bastard," Abe breathed out, and he took a single step

forward.

Mason met him halfway. Arms crushing each other tight, Abe tipped Mason's chin back and took his mouth.

Relief, joy, love, anger. It was all there between them, but Abe let it go the second Mason opened his mouth and invited Abe inside.

Just the taste of him was enough to strip away the years, the pain, the frustration and anger. Mason was real, he was here. They existed in this tiny pocket of time, untouched by reality.

Mason moaned into his mouth, and Abe tasted him deeper, hands rising to cup his face and tip his head, deepening the kiss. Mason wrapped his arms around his waist and leaned into him, pressing their hips together, legs settling in a tangled weave of limbs. Mason was real, warm, skin smooth and stubbled cheeks felt divine under his palms. Mason was heat and hard muscle and a sexy sweet layer under the brash exterior, and every time Abe kissed him, the armor fell away, revealing the wounded and kind soul underneath. It was as if Mason was incapable of hiding who he really was when they kissed, when they touched, but Abe didn't care why, he only enjoyed and treasured the change.

The real Mason was someone who rarely saw freedom.

Mason kissed as if he would never get the chance again. Desperate, needy, full of gasped whimpers and pleas for more. Abe gave him everything, hand sliding into his hair, pulling his head back and taking his mouth again. Their kisses were unending, neither stopping, taking small sips of air as they had their first real taste of unfettered passion in decades.

Abe lost track of time. Mason always did that to him.

Whether he was twenty-five or forty, Mason absorbed his whole focus the second they touched.

"Oh!"

The startled gasp behind them quickly gave way to giggles. Mason pulled back, giving Abe a look full of heat and promises, and Abe rubbed his thumb over his lower lip, wet from their kisses, before letting Mason go.

Percy stood a few feet away, sweet face full of smiles, blue eyes alive with joy. He giggled again when Mason rolled his eyes at him, and the tiny breeder sprinted forward, rushing the blood prince. Mason caught him, a pleased and surprised look on his face, and he hugged Percy in return.

"Mason! Mason! You're okay! Oh! But you're not! I'm sorry, are you hurt? You are hurt! Edward! Mason's hurt!" Percy's chatter was fast and ebullient, and the usually shy Percy was overcome with joy and flash pan concern.

"I'll live, little mouse," Mason replied, gently easing him back. Now that Abe wasn't kissing his brains out, he could see the cuts and bruises, the way Mason moved stiffly. His face bore marks from fists and boots, though faded by a few days. From the way he moved, Abe didn't doubt that his prince was covered in half-healed wounds.

Mason cupped Percy's face, his eyes so bright, luscious pink lips curved in a shy smile, a blush on his cheeks. Mason put a hand on his stomach, where the baby bump was poorly hidden by his shirt and jacket.

"Are you well?" Mason asked, and Abe could tell that Mason meant both Percy and babe in that question.

"We are," Edward answered instead, coming out from the trees, gently tugging Percy out of his brother's arms. "I've told you time and again, Mason—stop touching my mate!"

"He's so adorable Eddie, I can't resist," Mason quipped, but whatever he was about to say next was broken off by Edward throwing himself forward.

The brothers held each other. Abe so rarely saw them interact that each time was a surprise. Edward clung to his older brother, and in that clutch of arms Abe could see just how hard Edward was holding on. Always so in control, the capable and dependable prince was reduced to a young man who wanted, who needed, to lean on his big brother.

Mason held Edward as if he would change his mind and pull away, squeezing the younger prince to him. Edward chuckled, and pressed his face to Mason's shoulder. Abe very politely pretended not to see or hear the few tears that snuck out from princely men, and he went to where little Percy was hovering. Percy was crying, unashamed. The little breeder was one of the most emotionally honest people Abe had ever met, and he recalled Edward's words to him the other day. Anyone who was bothered by Percy's tears would quickly find themselves crying for another reason, and it was bound to be a painful one. No one messed with Abe's friends...his family.

Abe gathered Percy in his arms, and Percy gave him a startled glance, but snuggled in for a hug. Abe let him sniffle and wipe at his tears in peace, no judging. Percy was small, but lean, finely muscled, and he was a joy to hold. Abe held Percy in the shadow of his taller frame, sharing his warmth as the brothers reunited.

Mason was whispering in Edward's ear, but he was too far away to hear what the elder brother was saying. Edward gave a short, jerky nod, arms hugging Mason all the tighter before falling away. Mason wiped his brother's cheeks with his thumbs, and Edward kept his back to Abe and Percy, as if embarrassed.

"The palace is going bare for heirs, with both of us out here now," Edward said, words full of tears, and he coughed, clearing his voice. "Is Malcolm wandering in the wilds too, or is he still following Father?"

"Father has only one heir, and Malcolm knows better than most exactly who that is," Mason replied, dark eyes on Edward's face. "He'll fight for what best interests him, as always."

Abe tightened up all over. Surely Mason didn't mean… "Is it time, Mace?" Abe asked quietly, Edward looking back and forth between them.

"Time for what?" Edward demanded.

"Time to tell the truth, and free us all," Mason said. "But not outside, in a damn squirrel's parlor. There's a far warmer and more enjoyable place we can share our fireside tales, and I need to put my feet up. I've been tortured you know, and hunted like a dog for days."

Percy gasped in sympathy, and Mason sent the small man a wink and a smile before heading back towards the station. "Where are you going?" Edward asked, motioning back over his shoulder. "We need to get out of here, Mace."

"You can head for the border, brother, and I'll wish you luck. But fifteen-hundred miles of cities and forests and towns full of avid royal watchers is between you and freedom. Be realistic. Getting there might happen, but the traveling isn't wise, not so encumbered." Mason tipped his head at Percy's belly, and Edward narrowed his eyes.

Before Edward could lay into Mason, Abe stepped up and

put a hand on his shoulder. "Mason and I can protect Percy better than an entire army of Elysian soldiers," Abe vowed, and Edward sent him a searching glace, jaw tight. Mason continued walking, leaving him to convince his brother. "He knew we would be here. Perhaps not exactly, but he came this direction because getting to Elysian may be the best chance for Percy, but it isn't the most likely of plans to succeed. We'll all be safe if King Henry is stopped, and running away won't be necessary."

"And he wants us to go where, exactly?" Edward asked, frustrated.

Mason roared back in their direction, stopping the bike a few feet away. "Lord Estiary has been the most gracious host," Mason said over the rumble of the bike's engine, "And I warned him his involvement might mean a death sentence instead of banishment, but the crazy old badger just laughed and reached for another glass of wine. I'll see you at his estate. Want a ride, little mouse?"

Percy squeaked in alarm, eyes wide as he stared at the bike. Mason laughed when Edward grabbed Percy's arm and stood in front of him. Abe waved Mason off, not wanting the brothers to start digging at each other so soon. "I'll get them there, Mace. Go, I'll see you soon."

Mason revved the engine, the bike taking off in a flurry of sprayed dirt and leaves. Abe watched as the love of his life disappeared into the forest, the roar fading as Mason got further and further away. One day soon they would be able to just... stop, and be, and exist only in each other.

If they lived, that is.

Lunatic kings and misplaced heirs needed to be settled

first, though, before love could find time to flourish.

"And if Estiary makes a move for Percy?" Edward hissed, dark eyes full of violent promise at the possibility.

"Then we can be on the run for killing a noble, too," Abe assured the prince, walking back towards where they hid the SUV in the woods.

CHAPTER SEVEN

Percy

FINDING HIS courage, Percy held Edward's hand, chin up, shoulders back. He walked next to his lover, and not behind him, no matter how badly he wanted to hide in his shadow. Mason stood at the top of the stone steps of the great manor hall, the wind whipping his dark locks in a rather heroic manner. The dark clothes he wore merely completed the look, and one glance at Reynard's countenance told Percy that the captain was deeply affected.

Seeing Reynard and Mason kissing had been one of the most beautiful and surprising things of his short and sheltered life. Just the amount of love and passion in how they touched each other made Percy want to hug them both and sigh over them at the same time. He was rather emotional about it, and he glared down at his baby bump just as they escaped the wind and entered Lord Estiary's home.

Mason fell back to Reynard's side, and Percy smiled, thinking the two tall, powerful men were stunning side by side. Edward squeezed his hand, and Percy sent him a guilty glance and a shrug at his questioning look. Edward flicked his eyes at his brother and guard, and his brows twitched and his lush lips quirked in a smile. Edward put his arm around his shoulder and hugged him, following Reynard and Mason as they walked down an impressive entrance hall.

It was at least three stories tall, with twin staircases rising from either side. A balcony joined them over the main hall that disappeared into the depths of the mansion. The building was huge with rich rugs and tapestries on the walls in vibrant hues and scenes. Everywhere Percy looked were gold accents, and instead of the red of the Cassian décor, there were deep, royal blues, twilight hues and ocean shades. Percy was awed, and the effect was that of cool, calm welcome, despite the grandeur.

Percy was slightly confused. They had yet to see any servants. Mason had opened the front door on his own, and they entered alone. There was no waiting servant to greet and guide them to their host.

The four of them walked deeper into the house, the thick stones walls and the hues of blue making it feel colder in the shadows. Bright lights and the sound of music could be heard ahead, and Percy picked out the tinkle of high pitched giggles and deep masculine laughter.

Edward's arm went tight around his shoulders, and Reynard dropped back to walk on Percy's unprotected side. Mason shot them a quick glance, sarcasm having an expression it would be in the way Mason shook his head at them. They stopped outside the open door, golden light spilling over them.

Percy peeked around Mason's wide shoulders, eyes going wide at the sight in front of him.

It was a large room, made for comfort, couches and chaises and lounges littering the expanse. Wide loveseats and deep piles of pillows completed what Percy would compare to a harem from his fantasy books, and when he saw the nearly naked and beautiful forms lounging about, he figured it was pretty accurate.

"Dammit, Mason! I didn't want him in this environment!" Edward hissed at his brother, and Percy found himself behind Edward, view obstructed.

"Eddie, Percy grew up in this environment. We're the ones out of place, not him," Mason said casually, and Percy looked around Edward to see Mason shaking his head. "There's nothing to be scared of, Eddie. Your precious virtue is safe from some fluff-brained pleasure slaves and a handful of retired breeders. Oh, and an aging harem master, but he's too drunk to bite hard."

"Mason!" Called out an accented and slightly slurred man from inside the room, and the giggling cut off. "My darling boy, did you find your lost love? Ah, I see you did! And is that Farmer Eddie I see? Tell the young prude to stop being so jealous of his lovely dove, I have plenty of my own. Come in, gentlemen, and have a drink!"

"Prude? Did he call me a prude?" Edward asked angrily, and Mason laughed. "Farmer Eddie?"

"Coming, Lucius," Mason called out, and he walked inside the room.

Percy waited for Edward to make up his mind. Reynard stopped halfway between Mason and Edward, as if torn, waiting as well for Edward to make a decision.

"Saint's Blood....." Edward grumbled, but he took Percy's hand again and walked forward. "Percy, stay at my side at all times, understood?"

"Yes, Edward," Percy promised, following.

There were at least twenty people in the room, with maybe enough clothes between them all to cover a normal sized man. Percy was accustomed to nudity, in himself and others, and the naked pleasure slaves and the rare breeder he could see didn't bother him at all. The slaves were easy to tell apart from the breeders, at least for Percy. The slaves, all females, were lithe and slim with an elfin cast to their features, with high, smallish breasts and narrow waists. The breeders, also female, had wider hips and more flesh on their waists, though they were by no means overweight. The breeders also bore marks of their purpose, faint silver stretch marks on stomach and waist, and breasts that were fuller and not quite as high. The pleasure slaves were sterile, and their attributes were decorative, and unchanging until advanced in years. Breeders aged, albeit slower, but they still showed themselves to be past the first blush of youth. Percy only ever saw breeders past the age of thirty when they were retired back to Heritage and taken to the breeding pools to continue the in house stock lines, so to see the handful of females free to move about and not pregnant was odd for him.

Edward led him after Reynard and Mason, who were taking seats near the fireplace, where an exceptionally handsome older man was holding a clothing optional version of Court.

He was clothed, but the pretty slave on his lap was not. She was tiny, and looked no older than Percy, but she was designed to look that way, and could be ten years older. Wild, long and bouncy curls of vibrant red hair spilled over her shoulders, and deep blue eyes, almond shaped and fringed by thick black lashes gave her an angelic air, but her bare, perky breasts and legs open invitingly dispelled quickly any hints at innocence.

Percy took in their host, his silver hair thick and swept

back from his forehead, with a slight widow's peak and dark eyebrows over gray eyes gave him a very distinguished appearance. He was wearing black trousers and a deep blue waistcoat, a white shirt underneath open at his throat. He was older, perhaps in his fifties, but he was lean and his arms, the sleeves rolled back, were muscled and toned. Rings glittered on his fingers, and Percy politely looked away from the hand that was buried between the red-haired slave's legs, making her pant eagerly as he worked a finger in and out of her wet pussy.

Edward sat in a high backed chair, and Percy went to curl up on the cushion on the floor at his feet, but Edward pulled him to his lap instead. Percy curled up, tucking his feet under him, and he stared back at the older lord, meeting his inquisitive gaze.

"Greetings, assorted princes and guard," Lord Estiary said with a wave of his free hand, his other still moving with purpose between the slave girl's legs. "And a most hearty welcome to the beautiful Perseus, royal consort."

Estiary picked up a crystal and blue-gem goblet from a tiny side table beside his throne-like chair, sipping the deep red liquid from it, gray eyes roving over Percy where he sat in Edward's lap. Lord Lucius moved his fingers in a smooth glide over the girl's clitoris, and she came with a mangled scream, convulsing on his lap, legs closing on his hand, her breasts quivering as she struggled to breathe past her orgasm. Lord Lucius just sipped his wine and slowly withdrew his hand, making the exhausted girl spasm one more time before she sleepily rolled off his lap. She grabbed a folded cloth napkin from the small table, and handed it to her master who put down his goblet and cleaned his hand. She took the napkin and walked off, all without looking at any of them where they sat nearby.

"Lord Lucius," Edward began, but the older man waved a hand and sat up straighter, gesturing to Percy.

"He's Cartwright's design, isn't he? I recognize the eyes, Cartwright kept him in his study like a puppy when he was knee-high. About a decade ago, so the age seems right." Lord Lucius smiled at Percy, thin lips curved ever so slightly, and Percy looked away, refusing to show the aging harem master any emotion. "Cartwright named him Perseus, after a hero from a faraway foreign land. As I recall, it was the boy's favorite tale, and Cartwright read it to him often."

He didn't remember Lord Lucius Estiary, but it was possible they'd 'met'. Cartwright, Percy's designer and creator, had indeed kept Percy in his study when he was little, letting him read and play by the fireplace. As a child Percy was allowed a simple cotton shift and sandals, and Cartwright taught him to read in between client meetings. Cartwright never let Percy be alone with clients, and kept them all away from him, prohibiting contact. His late master was dead, dying a month before Edward visited Heritage and bought him.

"Percy is off limits, in all ways," Edward said directly to Lord Lucius, and Percy looked down at the floor, tensing. "You'll not speak to him or about him, Lord Lucius."

"Bold words for a disgraced prince," Lord Lucius said, sipping his wine. "And what a way to treat the breeder you collared for love. I know full well Cartwright didn't inhibit his mental development like he did with his regular stock. Young Perseus understands every word I say, and has the brains to speak his own back to me."

Percy froze, not daring to look up, either at Edward or at Lord Lucius.

"Percy is not up for discussion," Edward growled, all but vibrating under Percy in the chair, anger in every tense line. "He has nothing to do with why we are here."

"Don't think me a fool or a drunkard, your highness!" Lord Lucius all but shouted, standing swiftly, towering over them. Reynard stood just as fast, coming to stand at Edward's shoulder. "Your mate and the babe he carries is what this is all about. Everything depends on that babe he carries, of oh-so-pure Cassian decent. King Henry has let greed and fear cloud his mind, and when he realizes very soon what he has let slip through his fingers, there is no place on the planet you'll be safe. And once Mason finishes telling his tale, the whole of the country will be demanding your child."

"What the hell is going here?!" Edward demanded, and he stood. Percy found himself passed to Reynard like a parcel, and the guard held him protectively in his arms, backing away as Edward got right up in the noble's face. "You'll explain yourself, and now. I don't mind adding assault to the charges of treason I'm certain my father has placed on me. Speak, clearly, and now."

Mason sighed in his chair, the only one of them relaxed and not standing. "Eddie, shut the hell up and sit down. I'll start talking. And for Saint's sake, Luke, stop goading my baby brother. He is unreasonably protective of the little mouse. He just might do it, and I'm of a mind to watch."

Edward kept glaring at the nobleman, and Lord Lucius cracked out a burst of laughter before calmly backing away and sitting. "Very well then, Prince Mason. You have the floor. I delight in seeing what our youngest blood prince thinks after we have full disclosure of the sordid facts."

Edward

EDWARD BREATHED in deep, remembering who he was, and who he didn't want to be. Reason, calm, control. He was all of these things. He wasn't the entitled crown prince, who sulked when he didn't get the choicest meat, nor was he the brash and rude middle son, who made it a point to need no one and make sure they knew it. He saw the flaws others hated most in his brothers and made it a point to be more, and yet less.

Who was Edward, third son of the king? Farmer, tax law expert, master, lover? Father? He looked at Percy, his lovely mate held securely in Reynard's arms, the captain ready and willing to give his life to protect Percy's. His mate, whose ice-blue eyes were fraught with worry and tension, all but begged him to find peace.

The control he'd been struggling with the last weeks was all but gone. So used to having his life be the way he wanted it, undisturbed by politics and family backstabbing, Edward realized with a harsh awakening that he was spoiled. He was a prince, cast adrift in world he couldn't control and he certainly could not protect his mate and unborn child. He relied on Reynard to protect them from harm, and even Mason, the seemingly crass and degenerate rake, had more value and skill than he'd given him credit for, and was immensely more suited to the life they were living than Edward was.

In that epiphany he realized he was no one. Yet he could be someone, and he wanted to be more than what the world saw, and what he had been before. Every moment set before a man he had the chance to be better than he was before, and that thought sent the tension from his body.

Edward relaxed, and sat. He would listen, and learn, and then figure out what kind of prince he really was. What kind of man. Percy made a small movement from Reynard's arms, but Edward glanced up at the captain who nodded and sat back down, holding securely onto Percy. His mate gave him a small moue of his lips, and Edward sent him an apologetic smile before returning his attention to their host.

"Apologies for the outburst, Lord Lucius. I have no excuse for my behavior." Edward had plenty of reasons, but he refused to act the child. That was Mason's job. Lord Lucius gave him a gracious nod, and Edward glared at Mason. "Speak up, brother."

"Oh, is it my turn?" Mason asked, leaning back in his seat, legs crossed, looking so alike Reynard that Edward wondered just how far back their liaison went.

"Mace," Reynard warned in a soft tone, and surprisingly enough his brother sat up in his chair and lost the insouciant attitude.

"First begin with why Father is listening to the Minister of DNA Engineering and Cloning," Edward said. That was the most pressing matter—the why would explain how the king could be bent to follow the wishes of a single minister, a minister who was appointed by the king, and not the people. All their father had to do was dismiss the minister and appoint someone new. For the king to let a mere minister, no matter how influential, to meddle in the affairs of the royal family was almost unthinkable. "Tell me why he endorsed this manhunt and is coming after Percy. Malcolm said it was money, that the slave trade in Cassia is losing too much money for a breeder like Percy to be bound to one man."

"Well, cut to the heart of the whole fucking mess, why don't you," Mason muttered, incredulous. "You always were so smart, Eddie."

"Mason!"

"Fine. The illustrious King Henry the Third is being blackmailed, and bribed, by the Minister of DNA Engineering and Cloning."

"What?"

"Before he was the minister, he was a lowly geneticist and manipulation expert at a semi-well known breeding house. Goes by the name of Heritage Breeders, I'm sure you've heard of it. His name is unimportant, but he worked alongside a Master DNA Architect named Cartwright. That's not really important either, I'm afraid, just shows what a small world this is."

"Mason!"

"Ok, okay. This all boils down to our dear mother, Eddie."

"What does Mother have to do with anything? She's been dead for twenty years!" She died when Edward was ten, after complications from the birth of his youngest sister. That was what his father told him and the rest of the world, at least.

"Mother was ill, Eddie. She born sick, and she didn't tell

Father until after she had you. It's that disease that eventually took her from us, and drove Father mad."

Mason's face was set in stone, dark eyes a bottomless pit of pain. Edward stared at his brother until it felt like no one else was in the room, everything narrowed down Mason. Air seized in his lungs, his hands gripped the arms of the chair, and his legs tensed. He locked eyes with Mason, and said, "Keep going."

"A congenital disease that remains dormant until triggered by a childhood illness, so only about half of the people who have it develop symptoms. It has a long and boring scientific name, but it's responsible for the winnowing of several noble houses around the world. It affects the reproductive organs and cells, more seriously in women. In men, it makes us sterile. Mother died because Father found out, and in an attempt to hide the illness from his country and ministers, he made Mother continue to bear his children through IVF and assisted birth. The line of Airric can have no weakness, and he believed more children would guarantee the continuation of our line, and hide the truth from any curious observers."

"I don't...." Edward was falling apart. He understood the words, the meanings, but in the context Mason was supplying he was lost.

Mason must have seen it in his eyes, as he got up and walked to him. Edward sat back and turned to his brother as he crouched beside his chair.

"Eddie, just listen. Mother was sick, before she married Father, she knew, but the King of Elysian wanted a marriage covenant with Cassia, so she married him anyway. She had Malcolm, then me, and then you, all of us naturally conceived and born. But she got very sick after you were born."

"I remember the servants talking about it. They said it was pneumonia."

"No, it was her disease. She got so sick Father called in specialists, and they found the disease. Father went to the best geneticists in the country, one of whom is now the current Minister of DNA Engineering. They all told him the same thing—that the disease was incurable, but it could be managed properly with the right treatment. Father lost it, to put things mildly. He married a woman who polluted the Cassian Dynasty with a fatal weakness, and that was something he could not tolerate. As a result, he had the three of us tested."

That made sense. If it was congenital, then they could have it. But what did that have to do with what was happening now?

"Malcolm and I have it, Eddie. You don't. It skipped you completely. You don't even have the recessive for it, so you can't give it to your child."

"Thank the Saint's," Eddie breathed out, his relief at that assurance enough to snap him out of his state of disbelief. Their baby wouldn't have it. "But Mace—you and Mal?"

"It affects men differently, little brother. In men, all it does is eventually render us sterile by destroying our ability to produce viable semen. Malcolm and I were both sterile by the time we were fifteen."

"You both have children," Edward stated, confusion returning.

"I'll explain that part of this whole mess in few minutes. Back to what happened after Father found out, okay?"

"Fine, keep going!"

"Father lost it, like I said. As punishment for not telling

him before the marriage, he forced Mother to continue to have children, even though she got weaker and weaker after each pregnancy and birth. She was unable to conceive naturally, so Father made the geneticist from Heritage Breeders impregnate her through IVF. She then delivered via C-section, because she wasn't able to deliver them naturally after you were born."

"This is insane."

"Yes, it is, because Father is insane. No normal, sane human being would do anything like this," Mason said, putting his hand on Edward's arm. "I'm almost to the good part, so hold it together."

Edward breathed in deep, and nodded, letting the air out slowly.

"Father got rid of everyone who knew. About the disease and Mother's forced pregnancies and the IVF and about Mal and I having it. He pretended there was nothing wrong, and he let Mother die from her disease. Everything was kept a secret. He let the geneticist live, and eventually made him a minister, just in case the disease worsened in any of us. And not because he loves us, Eddie, not really. Because he didn't want to risk the truth getting out. The line of Airric is supposed to be all but infallible, and the woman he marries almost destroys his house. It was never her fault, but he's insane."

Mason gripped his wrist, squeezing hard.

"Years go by, and the world knows no different. Mal knows because of the testing. I know because Mother told me the day she died, and I read all the journals she kept. Things were held in a horrible pattern of deceit and threats and betrayal, right up until the random day you decided you wanted to be a daddy."

Edward's eyes went to Percy. Thick, long reddish brown hair and ice-blue eyes, set in a face both handsome and pretty, part of a body that was graceful and strong. Perseus was the epitome of perfection, and yet it was the mind and heart under the physical perfection that enticed Edward and beguiled him. It was the human man under the designer body that Edward fell in love with, and it was with a horrible pang that Edward realized that he was not a decent person.

If he had chosen a different breeder that day, if there hadn't been an error on Heritage's part that day and Percy never made it into the show room, then Edward would have bought a different breeder, fucked it until it bore him a child, and he would have retired it to his estate like an old pet until he wanted another child. Edward would have gone on with his life, and never once given a thought to just how wrong it was that people were made for the selfish use of others, stunted in growth and mental acuity, and forced to breed. Even the pleasure slaves were designed to have no free will and be driven by sexual needs, and any thought to the potential of the human being under the sex was never once considered.

He never thought about it. He was never cruel to the few slaves he'd met, and while he was curious, he never bothered to understand. It didn't affect him or his life, so it didn't matter. None of it mattered until Percy.

"I see you're about to fall apart, but I need you to listen to me, Edward. You can fall apart in your misplaced grief and guilt in a few minutes, but I need you to listen to me now."

"I'm listening," Edward whispered, eyes on Mason because if he looked back at his lovely mate he would indeed fall apart.

"When you took Percy home, when you fell in love with him and then collared him, you forced Father's hand. He would have let you have any breeder but Percy. The proprietor of Heritage went to his old buddy, the Minister, and then the Minister approached Father. He told Father that if Percy wasn't returned, then he would leak to the press the whole sordid ordeal with Mother, Mal's and I's sterility, our sisters' birth. All of it. He promised Father that he would replace Percy to appease you, give Father a part of the profits from cloning and breeding Percy to produce more like him, and in return nothing would be revealed about the disease that leaves Mal and me out of the line of succession."

"Mason, dear God…."

"So that is what brought us to this current situation. You failed to turn over Percy and got him pregnant. I failed to keep my mouth shut and toe the line like I had the last twenty years, so I was beaten and tortured. The people I loved were finally out of harm's way, so I was getting my punishment instead of them. Percy needs to go back to Heritage, but not until he births his baby. Father needs your child. Because he failed to return Percy to Heritage, the truth can be revealed at any time, and everyone will know. Father can't have that. He needs your child as a back-up plan to the truth getting out. He would take you, but he knows now that controlling you is as pointless as controlling me."

"Mason, are you saying…"

"Mal is sterile. He cannot sire heirs. So am I. Our children are not ours, but our father's bastards. Neither of us can continue the line of Airric. Our sisters cannot inherit because of the laws put in place almost a century ago, prohibiting artificial conception to protect Airric's line from foreign DNA in a coup attempt. Only a Cassian conceived naturally can inherit, and that royal must be able to continue the line. The only Cassian Royal in the direct line of succession who meets all the criteria is you, and through you, your unborn child."

Edward's mind was spinning. He could hear Percy demanding that Reynard let him go, that he wanted to go to him. He could see Lord Lucius laughing into his wine out of the corner of his eye. But all Edward could do was cling to his big brother's hand, and let everything he knew about his family fall apart in his mind and heart.

CHAPTER EIGHT

Percy

EDWARD'S EXPRESSION was horrible. Percy struggled, but Reynard held him fast, keeping him on the captain's lap. He wanted to go to Edward, to comfort him, anything. His lover was breaking apart, and he couldn't just watch.

"How..." Edward audibly swallowed, and Percy went still, listening. "Percy is a breeder, he was designed and created. Wouldn't that disqualify our child? Keep him or her safe from this?"

"The law was made before breeders became viable for sale. Though we could argue that Percy was born as he is, which is technically true, so he is naturally the way he should be. Regardless, there is a loophole in the royal inheritance laws for them, further assisted in this case because from what Lord Lucius has shared about Percy's history. That he can only conceive naturally, through sexual intercourse, and not artificial insemination. That means the babe he carries meets the criteria to inherit through you."

Edward shot out of his chair so fast Mason fell back on his rear. Percy found himself yanked out of Reynard's arms and in the air, Edward carrying him down the length of the harem. Slave girls shrieked in alarm and ran out of their way, Edward all but running. He could hear Mason and Reynard calling after Edward, but his master didn't stop. Edward carried him deeper into the mansion, down dark halls and through even darker rooms.

Percy knew that Edward was panicking. Edward didn't know where or what he was doing, but all he could do was run, and take Percy away from everything. Percy wrapped his arms around Edward's neck and kissed his jaw, his cheek, the corner of his mouth. He whispered he loved Edward between kisses, stroking his hair and hugging him close. Edward's arms loosened their iron-hold on him and Edward began to slow down.

"I love you, everything is alright. I love you, Edward. I'm safe, you're safe, the baby is safe…" over and over, he reassured his prince, kissing him softly, until finally Edward stopped.

They were in a dark room, with white stone walls and stone floors, bare but for a thick rug in the center and a few stray, dried leaves blown into the room from what looked like a forgotten arboretum. Light filtered in through the dulled glass walls, streaked with dirt and dust, dead trees left to dry out and rot. The door slid shut behind them, hanging listlessly on its hinges, swaying in the faint wind coming in from a crack in the glass somewhere.

Percy found himself aching for Hartgrove, and the lush inside jungle that Edward had in his home. Edward had taken him in the arboretum not long before they left Hartgrove for the capital, before their world started to implode. Percy remembered how happy Edward was, how happy they both were, and he wanted to be that happy again.

Edward stopped in the thick rug, breathing hard, and he gently lowered Percy to his feet. Edward clung to him, and finally fell to his knees, pressing his face to Percy's stomach, breathing fast, hands clutching at Percy's clothes.

Percy carded his fingers through Edward's thick hair, tugging on the strands. Edward's eyes were scrunched up tight, and he was shaking, full-body tremors through his solid frame.

"I love you, Edward," Percy said, playing with his lover's hair. "I can do nothing to help you, to fix this, but love you. I can't understand what is happening to you, what you're feeling or thinking. All I can do is love you, and promise to never stop loving you."

Percy went to his knees, and gathered Edward to him, his prince laying on the soft rug beneath them, face in Percy's lap.

"Do you hate me, little one?" Edward asked, voice broken.

Percy opened his mouth to deny it, but stopped. Edward was asking for a reason.

"Because you bought me? To breed me, and then set aside once you had your heir?" Percy asked, trying to feel his way.

"Yes," Edward gasped out, tensing, holding himself rigid, as if waiting for Percy to condemn him.

"No, not even a little," Percy said, and it was true. He never resented or hated Edward for his original purpose in going to Heritage.

"How can you not?"

Percy knew how he felt, but articulating it was another matter.

"I don't hate you. I don't resent you. I was born and raised to this purpose, and if not you, then Cartwright, or another man. There was no future for me that ended with me free from a master and without my belly filled by his seed. Not even if I was kept at Heritage to be cloned and bred, and you never came. You, Edward, are the only outcome for me that ends with me happy and loved."

"You sound so sure, Percy. So calm. Certain. How can you be?"

"I…" Percy gave Edward a rueful smile when his lover looked up at him, dark eyes framed by wet lashes. "Not talking a lot means I think a lot. I listen, and I reason, and I feel my way through things. I may not know much about the world and everything in it, but I know how I feel about you. I've accepted and been thankful for your desire to have an heir since the night you came to Heritage. Your original purpose brought us together, and gave me your love."

Edward was quiet, relaxing, easing out of his tight, panicked state. Percy kept touching him, gentle strokes over face and hair. "Weren't you afraid?"

"Of you?" Edward nodded. "Of course I was. But I also wanted you. So badly. And every time you scared me, or put your hands on me, you also gave me reason to trust you. To let go of my fears. Mason was right, you know. Your love cured my fears."

Edward laughed, weak and short-lived, but a real laugh. "Don't tell him, he'll never let it go."

"I won't," Percy whispered, smiling.

"Mason," Edward said, and then paused, breathing in deep. "If he's right about all of this, if it's all true…Percy, I cannot be king. I can't even keep you safe without help. All I know is how to make things grow and tax laws. I look pretty in the royal portrait, but I was never raised to be king. I just can't…"

"Sshhh," Percy hushed Edward, hugging his shoulders. "You are still Edward, blood prince, farmer and tax expert and lover of Perseus, the most absurdly named breeder in the world. You're a man, first and most important, and the one I love. The truth isn't out there right now. It may never be. There's just us right now, you and me. Let go, Edward, and rest."

Edward quieted. He breathed, slow and even, wide shoulders eventually lifting from their hunched position. Percy ran his fingers over the skin of Edward's neck to the lines of his jaw. His hair fell over his face, and Percy brushed it back, tenderly cupping his lover's cheek. He leaned down to kiss his forehead, but Edward tipped his face back, and Percy ended up kissing his lips, just upside down. Percy giggled, and Edward reached up and held him down, taking the kiss longer, a shade deeper. Percy hummed, happy, and Edward licked his lips before dipping deeper.

Edward let him go, and Percy sat back up, laughing. Edward chuckled, and pushed himself to a sitting position, rubbing his face. His hair was a mess and he was flushed, and look tired. He looked everywhere but at Percy, as if embarrassed. Percy reached out and put his fingers on Edward's chin, tipping his face back to Percy like Edward had done to him so many times. Percy smiled at his prince, and leaned forward, kissing him.

Gentle, teasing nips, Percy kissed his love. Edward smiled against his lips, pulling back every time Edward tried to deeper the kiss, before dipping back in and kissing him again. Edward chuckled, and reached out for him, hands on Percy's hips and pulling him onto his lap. Percy went, wrapping his legs around Edward's waist, his ass resting on the thick length hardening beneath him.

The mansion was quiet around them, the room cool, the rug soft and welcoming. Edward took his mouth, his commanding nature returning, and Percy shrugged out of his jacket and shirt, all without taking their lips apart. Edward's hands roved over his sides and back, his shoulders, hands warm and setting fire to his skin in their wake.

The air was cool but it didn't matter, he was burning up inside. Edward ran the flat of his hand down Percy's chest, over his belly, rubbing the firm swell. Percy gasped in his mouth, and whimpered happily when Edward sent his hand lower. His pants were opened, the zipper lowered. Edward's big hand slid under cloth to encircle his cock, and Percy threw his head back, arching into the touch.

Edward kissed his neck, mouth open, tongue tasting over his skin. Percy arched back even more, inviting more of his lover's touch, Edward's other arm supporting him. Percy was able to toe off his boots, and stood quickly. Edward's mouth was at level with his belly, and Edward kissed his stomach, hands tugging down his clothing.

Percy stepped out of his clothes, naked. He shivered from the cool, but Edward soon settled him back in his lap, having Percy straddle his hips, ass open to the rigid cock Edward freed with one hand. Teeth nipped at his nipples, and Percy jerked as a shot of pleasure ran from his chest to his cock.

Big, blunt-tipped fingers slid in his crease, and Percy wiggled in Edward's lap, trying to impale himself. He wanted Edward in him, needed it. He needed to wrap his flesh around Edward and hold him as close as he could, deep inside, where they were one person, no separation.

Percy put his feet flat on the floor and lifted up, squatting over Edward's cock, hard and fully erect, head glistening with precum. Percy was just starting to get wet, and he wanted the burn. He sank down on Edward, moaning in delight at the too-full sensation and the stretch. He slicked up Edward's cock as he sank lower, the tug of skin on skin becoming softer, easier.

"Love you, Percy," Edward gripped his hips and lifted him just a bit, sinking his body back down. "Ride me."

"Yes, Edward," Percy sighed, pushing Edward down to the floor, settling even deeper as Percy let his weight force Edward all the way inside of him. Percy kept his feet on the floor at either side of Edward's hips, crouching on top of him, ass full of throbbing cock.

Percy sat forward, and pushed Edward's hands away from his hips and down to the floor. He held them there, ass clenching on his lover's cock, and Edward smiled and nodded, putting his hands behind his head and watching. He thrust up, just a bit, and Percy bit his lip and moaned, taking his lover's hint. He rose up, slow and careful, then back down, enjoying the hard slide of hot flesh in his channel. Edward sighed with delight, holding still, letting Percy set the pace.

Percy put his hands on Edward's chest, and rode his lover, slow, deep, and thorough. Their eyes met, and Percy fell headlong into Edward's gaze, seeing passion and love in the dark depths.

He wanted Edward to feel how much he loved him, loved the man he called master and lover. Father of his babe. Edward was everything to Percy.

Mason

"WHAT HAS you so captivated, dearest Abe?" Mason whispered in his man's ear, peering over his shoulder into the room. The door was open just wide enough to see inside, and Mason grinned at the sight of the very naked, very delectable Percy riding Edward with absolute devotion in every roll of his slim hips. Percy's slim cock rose hard and flushed against his baby bump, and Mason was surprised by how…sexy the image of the pregnant breeder was. Edward certainly appeared to be enjoying himself. "Oh my, what a show. The little mouse has some delightful technique, doesn't he?"

"Mason, shush!" Abe hushed him, and pushed him away from the door. Mason tried to keep watching but Abe pushed him back even more, back to the wall. Mason grinned, ignoring the pain from his still bruised face and split lip. His injuries were healing, and he would be fine.

Abe was taller than him by a couple of inches, and Mason let his lover tip his head back, examining the fading marks on his skin. Strong hands cupped his face, holding him still, and Mason leaned back on the wall.

"Want to check the rest of me?" Mason asked, running his hands over his tight black shirt, lifting a bit of it at his waistband. Abe's eyes tracked the flash of skin and the depthless twilight blue glowed with heat.

"I will, but later," Abe told him, slapping his hip and making him jump. Mason grinned, and Abe wrapped him in his arms and pulled him in for a hard hug. Mason breathed in the fresh, invigorating scent of pure male that clung to Abe, the scent that was his alone and one Mason would never forget.

"I was worried, my prince," Abe whispered in his ear, and Mason held him tighter.

"I know. I was, too," Mason replied. "About you, I mean."

"I know what you meant." He could hear the smile in Abe's words.

"Come sneak away with me, I hear reunion sex is the best. Better than makeup sex," Mason urged, running his hands under Abe's jacket and palming his ass.

"Not while we're in Estiary's house, Mace. I don't trust the old man not to try anything with Perseus." Abe pulled back just a bit, staying in each other's embrace. "What is your plan, then? Burn down the lies of King Henry and see Edward take the throne?"

"You know me so well," Mason smiled. "Taking the throne will be entirely up to Eddie. Exposing dear ole Dad's perfidy is top of my life's goals, though. I'm ready for the next phase. Just got to hit upload."

"Lucius is letting you use his connection to the communications and internet grids. Why?" Abe asked him, arms tight around his waist. "What is in it for the old codger?"

"Revenge, my dear man. Served cold with a side of fuck off." Mason felt Abe jerk at the sound of Lucius' voice a few feet away. The old man was sneaky. Mason hadn't heard him either. "I get to see Henry topple from his throne of superiority, and all the Cassian skeletons of the last forty years will come to light. It'll be an absolute joy."

Lucius came out from the shadows in the hall, standing in the dim light spilling out of the partially open door of the room where low moans and gasps of pleasure could be heard. Lucius leaned over and took a long glance, gray eyes lighting up in enjoyment and appreciation. "Cartwright was a genius. Look at that lad's lines. Beautiful stock."

Abe was in front of Lucius in a flash, forcing the noble back a few steps and away from the door. "Perseus is off limits, Lord Lucius."

"I heard our future king the first time, Captain. I'll not risk my life for a taste of him. I'll look, but no worries. I have my girls for my needs."

Abe's look of disgust made the nobleman take another step back, just in case. Mason smiled, thinking Lucius wouldn't have to worry about Henry or Edward killing him, but Abe. "Lucius, do be careful. Abe is sensitive when it comes to breeders, and especially Percy."

"Ah, yes, I recall. The late Baron Reynard created quite a scandal all those years ago when he bought that male breeder. One of the first to be made, too. He even named it!" Lucius smiled. Abe's glacial demeanor was so full of subtle, thrumming violence that it filled the hall. "He bought it from Heritage, too, if I'm not mistaken. What a terribly small world. Does the young lad in there know you are the child of one of the first male breeders ever created, Baron Abelard Toussaint Reynard?"

"No, he does not," Abe breathed out, voice made of menace. "And you'll not tell him, either."

"Ashamed of your heritage?"

"Never."

"How strange then that you don't want him to know. No worries, I'll figure it out. I always learn the truth eventually."

"Which is why you were exiled in the first place, Luke. Maybe you should take a hint?" Mason said, and Lucius laughed at him.

"Good point, dear boy. Are you ready then? I can't wait to see how fast your next video hits the national news."

Mason took Abe's hand. "Come on, Abe. Luke has more security in this mausoleum than Father does on the Treasury. The house is secure, and you have the SUV keys. Eddie and the little mouse are too wrapped up in each other to get in trouble or run away. You can hover over them while they have sex—as I'm sure you've done before, you deviant—or you can come with me."

"And you'll be doing what?" Abe asked, but he followed Mason when he tugged on his hand. Mason twined their fingers together and Abe walked at his shoulder, like they did when they first met, all those long years ago.

"I made another video, but this one is special. I uploaded all the content from this," Mason held up the portable hard drive, and Abe's eyes went wide when he recognized it.

"That's the drive you stored all the information you stole from your father. Your sisters' medical records, the sterility tests for you and Malcolm, the paternity tests for Camilla's and Arianna's children, and Queen Esme's journals. I thought you said King Henry destroyed it years ago."

"I told you that to keep you safe from him," Mason confessed, pausing as they walked down the hall, turning to Abe. "If you thought it was still out there, you would have searched for it, and Father would have noticed. I couldn't risk you. Your decision to accept his offer to work in the royal guard almost broke my resolve! Abe, goddammit. It took too much to get you on Edward's protection detail and out of the capital to Hartgrove, I wasn't going to waste it all by having you hunt for the drive."

"I wanted to use it to free us both!" Abe hissed, blue eyes full of stifled anger and frustration. Mason sighed, and leaned his weight into Abe, trying to bring some comfort to his lover.

"I know. But Abe, sweetheart..." Abe's lips twitched at the endearment, and Mason grinned, "Abe, we are both free. Right now, totally free. In danger for our lives, but that's not so new for us. The freedom is though, and I'm going to use the drive to bring down the fortress of lies King Henry has built around himself and our family."

"Twenty years," Abe said to him, somber. Mason nodded, agreeing. Abe continued, his deep voice a sexy rumble that sent shivers down Mason's spine. "Twenty years I've waited to call you mine. Two decades of watching you bend until you broke to your father's will, his threats against me and Edward. Helpless to save you or stop him. I did everything I could short of murder to help you, keep you going. Though if it wouldn't have meant I'd be in jail for regicide, I would have killed Henry when you came to me as that scared fifteen year old, beaten and bloody for confronting his father."

"Mmmm...and let on to the world that I was dating a twenty year old soldier stationed at the palace barracks? Smart," Mason murmured, kissing Abe on his neck just below his ear. "That would have made everything sooooo much better. Arrested for regicide and statutory rape."

A hand landed in his hair at the back of his head, and Mason found himself trapped between the wall and all six-foot four inches of rock-solid former special ops soldier. He gasped, the grip tight, just this side of pain, and Abe put a hard thigh between his legs, lifting until he was pressing against Mason's groin. Mason went limp, letting Abe have his way, and his lover grumbled and pushed harder with his leg, lifting Mason an inch off the floor. Mason was sitting on Abe's thigh, his cock and balls firmly wedged against hot, firm flesh.

"I fucked you when you were how old, Mason?" Abe growled in his ear, nipping at the tender flesh he found there.

"I was…I was eighteen when you fucked me the first time," Mason gasped, trying to tip his head to the side so Abe could have better access.

"Mmm…..wasn't it your birthday present?" Abe bit down on the skin between shoulder and neck, and Mason's cock joined the fun, straining against Abe's leg.

"Best birthday ever," Mason agreed, melting into a puddle of liquid heat as Abe's free hand wandered down his chest, all the way to his waistband. Mason sucked in a breath, and Abe's fingers deftly opened his fly, and slipped inside. Abe palmed his cock, stroking it base to tip with his hot hand.

"Fuck," Mason swore, eyes rolling back at the pleasure swamping his senses.

"This is mine, Mason," Abe said in his ear, the words making him shiver. "Just as your heart is mine. Isn't that right, my prince?"

"Always yours," Mason agreed, as Abe's strokes grew firmer, more demanding. Precum oozed from the slit and Mason whined deep in his throat as Abe's thumb brushed through it, spreading it over the crown of his cock. "Body, heart, soul, all yours."

It didn't take Abe long to get him off. Mason missed his lover more than words could express, their lives a horrible mixture of quick, desperate rendezvous and snatched kisses in the palace halls. Too long denied Abe's touch, Mason came after a handful of strokes, Abe catching Mason's seed in his palm as it pumped out of him in thick, heavy spurts.

Mason was limp, muscles useless as Abe held him up, supporting his full weight. The hand in his hair let go, and Mason slumped forward, resting his head on Abe's shoulder, his arms dangling at his sides. He breathed through the aftershocks, and roused when he heard Abe groaning in appreciation. He lifted his head, and laughed.

"You really are a deviant fuck, Baron Reynard." Mason chuckled at the sight of Abe licking his fingers clean of Mason's spend, obviously enjoying the taste.

"But you love me, anyway, Prince Mason of the Blood," Abe kissed him, and Mason could taste himself on his lover's tongue.

"I do," Mason promised, and he found his feet under him again as Abe backed away.

"Are you boys done now?" Lucius' voice echoed down the hall from somewhere up ahead, and Mason laughed. "I'm too old to be loitering in drafty halls while you two…reconnect."

"We're done…for now, you old perv!" Mason called back down the hall, and he muttered to Abe, "Not like he wasn't watching the whole time."

"Was he really?" Abe said, eyes deceptively wide, and Mason fell out laughing at the guileless expression on his lover's face.

"What's so funny?"

They both turned to see Edward walking up behind them, Percy fully dressed and asleep in his mate's arms. The little breeder had a faint smile on his kiss-swollen lips, and the scent of sex was heavy in the air. Edward passed them in the hall, sparing Mason a quick glance as he went by. "Mace, do up your pants, I don't need to see what Reynard was just playing with."

Mason rolled his eyes and re-buttoned his waistband, and Abe wrapped his arm over Mason's shoulders. They followed behind Edward as they caught up to Lucius, Edward asking the noble for a quiet room for Percy to recover in.

CHAPTER NINE

Percy

PERCY OPENED his eyes to see the red-haired pleasure slave inches from his nose, her beautiful eyes wide with curiosity.

"Hello," Percy said, keeping his voice low. Pleasure slaves could be skittish, especially the females, their reactions to things and people exaggerated to create a more enthusiastic response during sex. He had very little interactions with female breeders once he hit puberty, but their mental development was stopped right about that time, so she would be relatively the same as the others he knew from his life at Heritage.

"Hi," she breathed out, voice a girlish mixture of awe and enjoyment. "Are you a new toy for Master Lucius?"

"No," Percy said, not unkindly, sitting up. He was dressed again, though he couldn't recall doing it himself. After he rode Edward until they both came he had very little recollection. He tended to pass out after sex. "I belong to Master Edward."

"Oh! He's very handsome," the red-haired slave gasped out, a delightful blush building on her cheeks, eyes twinkling. "Will we he want to try us, too? Master Lucius lets us share."

"Us?" Percy looked up, and saw that in the small sitting room where he was placed on a wide chaise, he was surrounded by the female slaves of Lord Lucius' harem. They sat clustered around the chaise, the red-head laying stretched out beside him, others sitting on the floor or peering over the sides, all of them watching him. Percy smiled at them, and he felt oddly out of place. He thought even that to be odd, since up until a few months ago, he was surrounded by slaves and breeders.

He swung his feet down, bare toes touching a thick, warm rug, and he stretched with his arms over his head, arching his back and moaning as his spine gave a few pops. Several gasps sounded from the chorus of slaves around him, and he lowered his arms and looked around, wondering what startled them.

A slim, tiny hand reached out, and Percy looked down to see the red-head rubbing his baby bump. She tilted her head like a bird, and the others all gathered closer, staring at his abdomen.

"You are a breeder?" She asked, coming closer, all but snuggling with him as she ran her hands over his baby bump, gently exploring. She was very naked, as were all the others, though her nudity wasn't what bothered him.

"Yes, I am. I carry my master's babe," Percy confirmed, and was about to lean back from exploring hands when she started to unbutton his shirt, pulling the sides apart. Warm hands on his skin made him jump, and he laughed, trying to back away, but he ended up pressed against the wide sloping arm of the chaise.

The females gathered in even closer, two brunettes climbing up on the chaise and crawling up on either side of him. They ran their hands up his thighs over his pants, sliding with curiosity over his groin before landing on the swell where his babe slept. Their hands were soft and warm, skin smooth and with delicate fingers, and they oohed and aahed over him with extreme interest.

"You are a male?" The red-head asked, sliding her hands down his belly, and Percy squeaked in alarm when she unbuttoned his waistband, opening his trousers. "A male breeder? Do you have a cock?"

"Yes!" Percy cried out, heavily startled, as the red-head went searching in his clothing. Slim hands cupped his cock and balls, and the two other slaves grabbed his trousers and tried pulling them off of him. "No! I belong to my master."

"Can we taste? Master lets us play with each other. Can we play with you?" one of the brunettes asked him, eyes guileless and a deep green, but her hands were anything but innocent as she ran them up his chest and pinched his nipples. He gasped at the sensations, and he blushed as his body responded to the stimulus, cock hardening in the skilled hands stroking him, his nipples hard little nubs as the brunette leaned over him and suckled on them. His body was designed to respond to sexual stimulus, and it rarely listened to his brain, if ever. He needed to get off the chaise and back to Edward.

"Stop! My master will be very upset!" In truth, Percy was getting upset himself. He saw now why slaves were separated at puberty. Sex would be all too common and unavoidable. The pleasure slaves were even more voracious than a breeder in heat.

Percy shifted on the chaise, trying to wiggle out from underneath the tangle of slim limbs and graceful forms. He was afraid to hurt them, and he could. While he was weak compared to Edward or Reynard, he was still stronger than these girls, and he could hurt them badly if he tried to force them off of him.

The two brunettes were all but sitting on him, and Percy tried pushing them away, and kicking at the chaise in an attempt to slide out from underneath the very eager girls. They were panting, flushed, and the scent of female arousal filled the air. Percy squirmed in earnest when the red-head knelt at his hip, hands on his hard cock, and she leaned down over her prize, mouth opening.

"I said no!" Percy shouted, startling them. The red-head pouted, her eyes narrowing, and she squeezed his cock. It leapt in her hand in response, and Percy hated his designer with a pure bolt of resentment in that moment. "Stop!"

The red-head smiled at him, and opened her mouth as she lowered herself down, fully intending to swallow his cock. Percy thrashed, and managed to get one of the brunettes off him. She fell off the chaise with a squeal of alarm, Percy rolled over, dislodging the red-head and sliding out from under the other brunette. He landed on the floor, and fast as he could he got to his feet, redoing his trousers and tucking his over-friendly cock back under his waistband.

"What is going on in here?" a stern voice demanded, and Percy froze instinctively, eyes down, hands at his side. That tone of voice was always the same, regardless of the name of the man who bore it or where he worked—a stable master.

The soft slap of leather on flesh made Percy peek. A big, swarthy man dressed in a simple cotton shirt and soft-looking silk pants wielded a golden chamois-wrapped crop, and he was spanking the red-haired slave girl on the ass with it. She moaned, lifting her ass as she fell to all fours, taking the whipping with pain and enjoyment. The stable master slapped her ass again, and she fell to her side on the floor, obviously enjoying the punishment more than not.

Percy risked a glance at the stable master as he waded through the slaves sitting on the floor, the girls ducking their heads and avoiding eye contact. The man was big, heavy-set around the waist and jowls, and his eyes were hard and narrowed as he caught sight of Percy staring at him.

Percy dropped his eyes and was about to step out of the room when the stable master pointed at him with the crop, freezing him in his tracks. Percy kept his head down and curled his hands to fists at his sides, wanting nothing more than to run out of the room and find Edward. Where was his prince?

"The master will be most displeased to learn you were in here, girls," the stable master warned, his voice scratchy, as if he spent more time screaming than actually talking. "He had the prince leave his breeder in here so he could sleep undisturbed. Return to the harem quarters. Now."

The girls scrambled to their feet, filing past Percy on their way out of the room. They were gone in a flash of shiny hair and pristine skin, leaving Percy alone with the stable master. He could see the big man approach, his house-shoes coming in view of Percy's downturned eyes.

"I shall have to inform your master of your trespass, breeder. Touching Master Lucius' property is against the rules. Sex without permission is worth a beating or two. Does he whip you or use a flogger?" The stable master may be asking, but Percy was too mad to speak. How dare this man think he was willing! He had no control over his body, and the response was automatic. He wanted no part of the female slaves at all, and they were the ones to accost him!

Percy glared at the man in front of him, lifting his head and meeting his gaze full on. "My name is Perseus, and my prince does not beat me. They touched me, and I told them to stop."

Anger swirled in the stable master's eyes, and he tightened his grip on the golden crop, making the leather creak. "Such insolence! Have you forgotten your place, slave? That collar about your neck doesn't make you less of a breeder or the prince's property! There are plenty of places I can punish you that would spare the heir." The stable master raised the crop, fast as snake, and brought it down just as quick.

Percy saw it coming, and in the first time in his whole life, dodged the punishment handed out by a stable master. The blow, meant for his upper chest, glanced off his left arm instead. It hit with a bolt of pain that made him gasp, but he kept moving. His arm went numb and tingled horribly, but he kept moving.

"You brat! I'll beat you bloody! I'll beat you so hard you drop that mongrel early!"

Percy ran, his bare feet finding plenty of purchase in the soft, luxurious rugs that covered the stone floor. He left the small sitting room, and found himself in a hall not far from the first room where they'd met Lord Lucius. Percy darted out of the way of the charging stable master as he barreled out of the room behind him, forcing Percy deeper into the house.

"Edward!" Percy shrieked as he ran, his cry bouncing off the white stone walls. The stable master was a couple strides behind him and closing fast. "Edward!"

There was a room just ahead, and he could hear men talking, their voices alarmed as they heard him screaming. "Edward!" he called again, weaker this time, his body still not used to running. He was fit, but lacked stamina, and his pregnancy left him alternating between exhaustion and cranky. If he didn't make it to Edward now the stable master would have him. Percy didn't doubt for a second that he was facing a horrible beating if the stable master caught him. His babe would not survive, not this early in his pregnancy.

Fear spurred him on faster, heart beating hard in his chest, lungs burning.

The stable master reached out for him with an angry shout just as Percy cleared the doorway. He saw Edward and ran full-out to his master, who caught him and spun him away from the stable master's grasping hand. Edward swung Percy into Reynard's arms, who caught Percy just in time for Edward to throw a nasty right hook directly to the stable master's jaw. The other man's momentum made him fly into Edward's fist, and the stable master slammed back first to the hard floor, head hitting with a thwacking sound so loud it made Percy flinch.

The stable master groaned in pain, but he was a big man and he shook it off, rolling to his side and then to his knees. Edward stepped forward and landed his booted foot directly in the other man's sternum, knocking him flat again.

Percy slipped out of Reynard's arms, and ran to Edward's side. His prince pulled him close, grabbing Percy's upper arms, concerned eyes sweeping over him. Percy knew he looked a sight; hair disheveled, shirt open and revealing his upper torso, and he was sweating from exertion. Edward's hand hit the spot on his arm where the crop hit him, and Percy winced, gasping in pain. Edward shot him a look, and lifted Percy's arm, revealing where the crop tore through the fine material of his sleeve and raised a thick welt on his upper arm. Blood beaded along the center of the welt, smearing as the cloth moved over it.

The rage that welled up in Edward's eyes was terrifying. Percy knew Edward had a temper, but he fought so hard not to let it escape him. The last time Percy had seen anger of this magnitude it was after the two footmen in employ of Heritage had insulted Percy in Edward's private quarters at Hartgrove. Edward barely let those two men live, and all they had done at the time was insult Percy.

Edward stripped Percy of his shirt, dropping it to the floor. He turned Percy so that the injury could be seen better, and the sounds that came from both Reynard and Mason, who was sitting nearby at a computer, made Percy flinch. Reynard moved to the stable master, but Mason jumped between them and grabbed the captain and held him back, whispering in his ear.

Edward gently, with extreme care, set Percy aside, out of the way. The stable master was getting to his feet again, and was reaching for the golden crop on the floor at his feet when Edward picked it up first. Edward let the stable master regain his feet, and he stood there, a belligerent and unrepentant expression twisting his face.

"Explain yourself, now."

The stable master glared at Edward, who was casually running his hands over the golden crop, testing the spring in its bend. "The breeder spoke out of turn. I punished him. I caught him cavorting with the master's slave girls. They had their hands and mouths on him, and he was enjoying it. Sex is not allowed unless the master gives permission."

"They accosted me, Edward, when I woke up," Percy said softly, refusing to let this nasty man pollute Edward's opinion of him. "I told them no, but my body...it did as it's meant to, and the slave girls were wrongly encouraged. I got away from them. The stable master came in and accused me. I corrected him. He struck me with the crop. I ran, and he threatened to... he threatened to beat me 'til I lost my babe."

"I believe you, little one," Edward reassured him, still holding the crop in his hands. He faced the stable master, who glared at Percy over Edward's shoulder.

"The punishment for assaulting a royal consort is death," Edward said, so very calm that it was even scarier than if he was screaming with rage. "You struck my mate, who is pregnant with my child. You then threatened the life of my babe. Twice then, that you earned death."

The stable master's face mottled with red and white splotches, anger, disbelief and some confusion marking his unpleasant features.

"Lord Lucius!" Edward called out, and the stable master tensed. He tried backing away, but suddenly Mason and Reynard were at his back, taking both his arms and forcing him to his knees. He was a big man, but both the prince and the captain held him fast.

"I'm here, my prince," Lord Lucius said from the far corner of the room, stepping away from another desk, this one full of computers as well, dozens of screens flashing with images. Lord Lucius came to Edward's side, and sent his gray gaze over Percy's arm. The blood was running freely now down to his elbow, and Percy's whole arm was throbbing, adrenaline wearing off, and he felt like he was going to be ill.

"He assaulted my consort, the bearer of my heir. He dies, by your hand or mine," Edward stated, and the stable master roared in anger, struggling against Reynard and Mason.

"I agree," Lord Lucius said calmly, "He won't see the dawn. I have texted my guards. Gentlemen, would you mind restraining my former employee until my men detain him?"

Mason grinned, and a knee came flying up, cracking across the back of the stable master's head. The man shouted and struggled, but both Mason and Reynard held him still. "Our pleasure. They can take their time."

Edward handed Lord Lucius the crop, who took it with a raised brow and a shake of his head. Edward came to Percy, and picked him up, carrying him to the fireplace, setting him in a chair. Percy could hear the stable master struggling, cursing as men in dark uniforms entered the room and took him away.

Edward's big hands gently cupped his arm, turning it so he could see the wound. Percy cried out, biting his lip, and blood dripped from his elbow, hitting the crushed blue velvet of the armchair he was in, beading. Percy started to breathe fast, feeling like he was suffocating, and he shook all over.

"Breathe, little one," Edward chided, as Percy stared at the blood, transfixed, even as his stomach fought to revolt. He really disliked blood. "Slow down, and in and out. Relax, you're safe now."

"It hurts," Percy whispered, wiping his face on his shoulder, Edward holding his left arm up and away from his body, blood dripping.

"I know, Percy. Reynard is right here, he has a first aid kit. Just breathe, and hold still, okay?"

"Okay," Percy said, and he looked away as Reynard joined Edward, the two men tending to his arm. He looked up as Mason came up to his right side, and sat on the arm of the chair. He was too big to do that, and Percy ended up with his face buried in Mason's hip, the older blood prince's hand carding through his hair.

Mason pet him, and Percy went limp, sniffling, and he gasped as his wound was wiped down, and something with harsh scent and a horrible burn was blotted over it. Mason tugged and pulled on his hair, distracting him, and Percy unashamedly cuddled with his master's brother, seeking comfort. Percy found himself picked up, and Mason sat down in the seat, and Mason settled him on his lap. Edward gave his brother a frown, but didn't say anything, and Percy cuddled as Mason wrapped him in a secure embrace.

Reynard cleaned the welt again, and then smoothed a salve over it. Percy could barely feel his arm below the welt, the pain was throbbing and his arm tingled. It was already bruising around the welt, dark purples and black building under his skin, and the white cotton bandage grew a red line through it as it absorbed more blood.

"Should we stitch it?" Edward asked Reynard, eyeing the bloodstain as Reynard wrapped Percy's arm.

"No, not with an injury like that. It's less a cut than it appears. Stitching won't stop the bleeding. It'll stop bleeding once Percy is settled down and he can rest."

"Always so exciting when you're around, little mouse," Mason said to him, and Percy looked up with a glare as Edward made sure his arm was clean.

"I'm not a mouse," Percy said, and Mason gave him a wide

grin.

"A kitten then, with tiny claws and sharp teeth," Mason said, and Percy all but passed out when Mason cuddled him in closer, kissing his brow. Percy felt a hand on his belly, and looked down to see Mason's hand petting his baby bump. Where having anyone but Edward touch him there bothered him, Mason's hand was warm and gentle, and he sighed.

"Are you alright with Mason, little one? I need to talk to Lord Lucius about what happened. I can stay if you need me to," Edward asked him. Percy knew that 'talking' was not what was going to happen. Someone was about to die.

"I'll be fine," Percy said quietly, pulling his arm to his chest and curling up now that they were done. "I'm sorry I caused trouble."

"You did no such thing, my mate," Edward said sternly, leaning down and kissing him. Percy kissed Edward back, and his mate pulled away after a moment with a sigh and a frown. "I love you."

"Love you too," Percy said, and Edward backed away from the chair, obviously reluctant to leave him, even with his brother. Percy gave him a small smile, and rested his head on Mason's chest. Edward sent a look at Mason, and Percy could feel Mason's chest shake with a soft chuckle.

Edward left, sending Percy another glance, Lord Lucius leaving with him. Percy refused to think about why they were leaving, or what was about to happen. He just couldn't think. His arm hurt so badly he wanted to sob, and he was tired. He drooped, spent and hurting.

All he wanted was a safe place. To just be safe, and be still, and settle. To rest and wait, and find the time to think about what his baby was going to look like. Boy or girl? With the Cassian coloration with dark, thick black hair and almost black eyes? Would any part of Percy go to his baby, or would the child be wholly Edward's, as was Percy's design?

A flutter came on the heels of that thought. Percy smiled, and closed his eyes. Mason's hand was still on his belly, and he felt it, too. His child stretched, and the movement, while still small, was significant.

"My niece is rather feisty," Mason whispered, rubbing his big hand over Percy's belly, chasing the movements as Percy's baby wandered a little.

"Niece?" Percy said softly, shivering. He was naked from the waist up, his shirt somewhere on the floor across the room.

A blanket came from nowhere, and Percy found himself wrapped up in a soft downy quilt, Reynard tucking him in and Mason pulling him back to his chest.

"Hmm, yes. A girl," Mason said with conviction, eyes bright. "I've always been able to tell. Haven't been wrong yet. Nearly thirty royal babies in the last decade, and I've been right every time."

Percy gave him an incredulous look, doubting it. It was more likely he snooped and found the sonogram results and then made a 'guess'.

"Ask Reynard if you doubt me," Mason said archly, smiling down at him. "And a lot of them were twin sets, and I got those right as well."

"No," Percy said, smiling back. "You must have cheated."

"I promise you, there was no cheating on my part. I have never seen a woman's personal bits that close, and I refuse to even contemplate that level of investigation."

Percy giggled, and Mason laughed with him. Some of the tension left his body, and Mason rubbed his belly, relaxing him some more.

"Is it true?" Percy asked, wondering if he should.

"What?"

"What you said before. About your children, about Malcolm's? Are they really...?"

"My father's by-blows? Yes, they are his, not ours. I shoot blanks, as the saying goes. And I have only ever slept with one person in my life, and it was most certainly not my witch of a wife."

Percy's eyes went to Reynard immediately, who was standing between the rest of the room and the chair where they sat. Reynard looked back at them over his shoulder, and gave Percy a small smile and a nod. Percy blinked, surprised. Mason seemed so....worldly, so rakish. A lifetime of fidelity to a single soul meant that there was more to Mason than Percy thought.

"I get Eddie on the throne, and the first thing he's doing for his favorite brother is annulling my farce of a marriage," Mason muttered, and Reynard's shoulders shook with a silent chuckle.

Percy blinked, confused for a second, and then what Mason said sank in. "You want Edward to take the throne?"

Mason looked down at him, brows raised, and he nodded. "By all rights, it's Eddie's throne. He is the only one of us who qualifies under the laws of inheritance for a Cassian Royal."

"But then..."

"Hhhmmm, that's true, little kitten," Mason murmured, making Percy scowl, "Your baby is the future king or queen of Cassia."

"I don't want…I didn't…think…"

"Whether he takes the throne or not, Percy, I am dethroning our father," Mason said, his conviction so strong Percy could feel it in his bones. "Whether he decides to exchange your freedom for a crown is entirely irrelevant to me. All I want is to destroy King Henry, as he's made me suffer for my whole life. He needs to be stopped. Murder, conspiracy, violation of inheritance laws, and arguments can be made for incest and reproductive assault, in the case of Arianna and Camilla. Hell, even my mother! For a man so devoted to the legacy of Airric, he's done nothing but pervert it for the last thirty years," Mason said, and Percy was captivated. There was a fire in the blood prince that shook him to his core. There, in that moment, Percy saw who Mason was under the armor and the bitter resentment.

If not for the silent disease that corrupted his body, Mason would have made a magnificent king.

"Mason," Reynard was at Mason's shoulder, concerned. "Peace, Mason. Just relax with Percy, alright?"

Mason frowned, and sent Reynard a narrow-eyed glare, but he nodded and relaxed. Percy gave Reynard an impressed glance. Mason ignored Edward when he told him to do something, but Reynard got an instant response.

Percy snuggled, determined to ignore the world and find some measure of calm. Mason's arms came back up and held him securely, and he felt safe. Not as safe as if he were in Edward's arms, but safe enough.

Mason

THE WAY Percy felt in his arms was odd, but pleasant. The little breeder was a light, easy burden to hold, the novelty of the baby bump was enjoyable. Percy didn't seem to mind, and Mason had never felt such a thing before. The tiny movements under his hands was tentative, almost shy, and then would settle down, as if the little one were napping.

Mason never touched his wife while she was pregnant. Hell, he never touched her, period. Ever. Arianna was a vicious hellion when pregnant, and she never offered, and he liked having hands, so he never tried. His sisters lived with their husbands on their estates, and he rarely saw them. Not that he was all that close to his sisters—they were so much younger than he, and after he learned the truth of their conception and birth, he had always been unable to be around them, the emotions too overwhelming and chaotic.

The children portrayed as his were a different matter. Camilla had them regardless of what Mason wanted. He'd never wanted children, at all, the desire absent in his heart. He was fond of children, he didn't dislike them, he just never wanted them. In some ways he resented them. Not fair to the younglings, since they were innocent in all this, but all he had to do was see them and feel every ounce of resentment and anger and bitter, burning impotence at his lack of choices.

He was forced to claim his brothers and sisters as his own children, and that was every kind of horrible fucked up lie. Mason had hesitated, for one second before he hit the upload button on his videos—the kids were not going to be spared. They would be protected, and sheltered from the reality of what was happening around them, of that he had no doubt, but the truth about them was out there right now, and King Henry's lies were being exposed one by one.

Mason looked up from the now sleeping Percy to watch the computer screens over Luke's desk. Every major news network was on, and several of the bigger online news vendors were up as well.

Mason had hit the button twenty minutes ago. And it was already happening. He had filmed a video, and in it he detailed the entire truth. From his mother coming to Cassia with the illness that eventually took her life, to King Henry's madness, the fathering of the royal bastards, to the threats used to blackmail Mason into marriage and reluctant fatherhood. He spoke again about Percy, who and why he was important, the pressure Heritage and the Minister was plying to the King, and the fact that Edward, Percy and Reynard were running for their lives. It was all there, including the revelations that out of all of King Henry's children, only Edward was the one qualified by blood and law to rule.

A video that took him over an hour to film, and with the video he put up the corroborating evidence from the hard drive he'd taken out of the hidden panel in Airric's throne. Years' worth of investigating and research and stealing evidence. All of it, everything Mason knew, and it was all out there in the world.

Mason had emailed it to every major news organization in the country, and the world. By morning, every single TV and computer screen would hold the truth.

Mason watched the muted screens. Evening dramas were cut short and interrupted by Breaking News alerts. Websites refreshed and new headlines appeared. One by one, within seconds and minutes of each other, Mason watched as the world received his message. It was out there, in the nether realms of the internet, and once it was released, the truth could never be erased.

He would give it a week or so, let the news be dissected and analyzed, let the palace deny and lie further. Let their father bury himself a hole he couldn't escape. Then, once it got to a fever pitch, he would use his greatest weapon yet.

Mason looked down at the young breeder in his lap. Percy was asleep, thick lashes curving over smooth cheeks, small hands curled into the blanket. Mason still had a hand on Percy's belly, and the tiny life danced under his palm. Percy slept through it, bandaged arm held stiffly, the welt and resulting bruising having spread even further. Mason indulged himself in the rage that came up in his core at the sight, and added it to yet another score to be settled.

Percy was slave. In this country, Percy was property. The greatest country in the world built and designed humans to be vessels for blood and pleasure, and be damned the morals twisted to achieve prosperity. The same with his own father, seeking to increase the prosperity of the Line of Airric.

Yet Percy was more than a mentally-neutered slave. He was whole. He was real, and he loved, and was loved in return. He was different, as the babe he carried could attest, but different didn't mean less.

Mason smiled, and dropped a small kiss in Percy's silky tresses. Now all he had to do was convince the others, especially Percy, to share with the world just how real they all were.

Love would defeat the king's insanity in the end. They just had to help it along.

CHAPTER TEN

Percy

"WATCH YOUR hands! Keep them up!" Mason heckled Edward as his prince and the captain circled each other in the empty ballroom. Both were shirtless, sweat dampened skin on display, and intent on beating each other into the stone floor. They had been at this for three weeks, the training, and Percy was ready to either go into labor early just to get them to stop or bury his head in a book until he was ready to give birth.

Percy winced when Reynard landed a vicious blow to Edward's side, making his prince double over, gasping for air. Reynard paused his attack, concerned, but then Edward came up and tackled his opponent, sending them both to the hard floor in a tangle of limbs. Mason cheered, encouraging the insanity, as Percy watched wide-eyed with near-horror.

Edward had been quiet in the last few weeks. Three weeks since his prince had left with Lord Lucius, dealt with the stable master, and come back to find Percy asleep in Mason's arms and the whole world going crazy. Percy woke that night in a quiet, dark room, wrapped in Edward's arms, his prince shaking and clutching him tight. Edward weathered a storm that night. Whether one of conscience or fear, indecision or regret, it mattered not, because the next morning Percy spread his legs for his prince, a man who was sadder, and there were tiny hints of lines beside his eyes, but he was man who was in control and resolute, and took Percy so thoroughly he felt it for days.

At times Percy saw a shuttered glimpse of some pain, a vulnerability that wasn't there before in his lover's eyes. Edward asked Mason question after question about the secrets his brother revealed, and how the country was taking the revelations. Edward approached Reynard, and asked him to teach him how to really fight. He claimed what he knew was bar room brawling from his university days, and he needed to know how to actually fight.

Some discussion was given about Percy learning to fight, but when he went green at the suggestion and almost threw up, that thought was quickly dropped. Instead he was lectured on how to fall, how to run, and the best places to hide if the crown came for them. It was only a matter time, Percy knew that, from the way the other men were acting.

Percy flinched as Reynard sent an elbow into Edward's jaw, and Mason's hands on his throat fell away. "Percy, hold still. I can't get this off if you're moving all the time."

"Sorry, Mason."

Mason was trying to pick the lock of the consort collar. It was rubbing him raw, despite the silk and salves. It was to the point where Percy was irrationally aware of the collar, and felt like he was choking, even though it was no tighter than the day Edward first put it on him. He loved the collar, he truly did, but his mind and body were rebelling at the silliest things as his pregnancy advanced, and he was beginning to wish they'd all stop being so damn careful and just cut it off of him.

He must have muttered that last thought aloud because

Mason gave him a stern look and a frown. "Bolt cutters won't work on the coils, Perce. The metal is too strong, and if it did manage to cut the coils, they would ricochet everywhere, and you'd be sliced to ribbons."

"But...." Percy whined. For the first time in his life, he was whining. Like a baby.

Percy sniffled, and Mason froze, eyes wide, hands stilled just before they returned to the collar's lock. Percy valiantly tried to withhold his tears, and when Mason stared at him like he was going to attack him Percy wailed.

"Why..." he sobbed, "Am I...crying?" Tears ran down his face, and Percy wiped furiously at his cheeks, eyes refusing to stop spilling.

He was tired and he wanted the damn collar off and he just wanted....he was fat! Percy looked down at his belly, which in the last week decided it wasn't big enough and had to get much bigger. Five months!!! Where were his five months to grow accustomed to being pregnant? Just then the baby moved, and Percy cried harder, since now he had to pee, and badly.

Percy got up, and walked away from the table at which they had been sitting watching the others spar. He sniffled, and when his ankles complained at the short jaunt down the hall to a restroom, Percy cried some more. He was so tired of crying!!!

He ended up sitting in a stall in the opulently adorned space, an overtly expensive square of toilet paper his tissue. He tried to get comfortable, but his hips ached, and his back ached, and he wanted nothing more than to have everything just stop.

A soft knock came on the stall door, and Percy could see

Edward's boots under the door. He sniffled, and got another piece of tissue, wiping his nose. "Yes?"

"Are you…" Edward must have sensed the glare he sent at his prince through the stall wall, since he amended his approach. "When you want to come out, I'll be waiting. No rush. I love you."

Edward's quiet and gentle declaration made him smile. Edward was trying so hard not to upset him further. Percy got up, and used the toilet, sighing in relief as his bladder emptied for what felt like the millionth time that day. He opened the door after he flushed, and gave Edward a small smile as he went to the sink, washing his hands.

His poor prince. Edward was bruised, shirtless, muscles gleaming with sweat, and he watched Percy like he was the most precious thing in the world. Percy dried his hands, and went to Edward, his prince folding him into a big hug. Percy kissed the firm swell of one pec, smiling when the small nipple there hardened in response.

Percy licked it next, and Edward jumped, groaning. "Little one, we don't need to…"

Percy ended that thought quickly by sucking Edward's nipple into his mouth, the tiny nub pebbling under his tongue. Edward sighed, big hands stroking his back and sides.

Percy went from crying to horny in seconds. He wanted his mate, his prince. The taste of salt on his tongue made him moan, cock hardening. Edward's hands ran up his back, his shoulders, and then back down, encouraging him. Percy touched every single inch of exposed skin, his own hands mindless in their desire to feel every edge and line of muscle.

Percy kissed his way up Edward's chest, standing on his

toes to get his neck. Percy licked then bit, hands on Edward's shoulders for balance, and he did it again, enjoying the silent hitch in Edward's breathing.

"Fuck me," Percy said, his breath ghosting over Edward's ear, and the whole body shudder that worked through his prince made Percy feel powerful.

Strong hands turned him around, and Percy gasped as his trousers hit the floor, his underwear soon following. His hands hit the mirror, and his feet were kicked apart. Edward pulled his hips back, and Percy was bent over, ass exposed and wet, cock throbbing in time with his rapidly beating heart.

The sound of a zipper opening and the slide of cloth to the floor made Percy pant with need. Seconds later hands spread his ass cheeks apart, and hot flesh pressing to his back and thighs left his head swimming with arousal. Edward wasted no time.

Edward's thick, hard cock was in him faster than his brain could process the sensations. Percy screamed, arching his back, pushing back against Edward as his master fucked into him, over and over. Percy's body went insane, his inner muscles trying valiantly to grip the cock spearing into him, but Edward's thrusts were too powerful, too fast, and so very deep.

"Harder!" Percy shrieked, and Edward gave it to him.

A hand gripped the nape of his neck, the other on his hip, pulling his body back as Edward thrust forward. Edward leaned over him, chest to back, and Percy mewled as the wet sound of their fucking joined their gasps for air.

"You are mine," Edward whispered in his ear, hot breath making him shiver even as the changed angle made his toes curl and his cock drip precum in copious amounts.

"Yes," Percy said, barely getting the word out. "Yours."

Percy came. Hard, deep, violently, he came over the wall, the mirror, and the floor. Arms lost their ability to hold him up, and Edward pulled him back to his chest, standing them upright, and Percy's inner muscles finally caught Edward in an impossible grip, sucking him in deep. Edward came with a shout, and Percy shattered in his arms.

Percy

PERCY WOKE up in the sitting room that Lord Lucius had converted into a type of computer room. Mason had commandeered a desk, full of flat screen monitors, and more equipment than Percy could name. He only barely understood exactly what the internet was, while he listened patiently to Mason explain it, he still ended up wishing for a book and warm cup of tea.

"...King Henry, my father, made it clear, that if I did not release Percy as my consort willingly that he would be stolen from me, and if I protested, that I would then meet an unfortunate end. When my father learned that Percy was pregnant, he threatened to steal my child as well, and I would never see Percy or my babe again."

Edward shifted on the stool the camera in front of him making him awkward, but Percy could see the anger underneath the embarrassment of the situation. Edward was a private person, and Mason's videos stripped away the layers, made everything accessible and exposed.

"My father is not the man he shows the world," Edward said, eyes locked on the camera, unwavering. He spoke with restrained anger, the unease at speaking thus fading away. "He cornered Percy, my consort, at one of the christening parties late last month. He tried to choke Percy, in a drunken attempt thwarted by my brother, Mason. He almost killed the man I love and our babe. My father's insanity has no limits."

Mason clicked a button, and the lamps that illuminated Edward on the stool went dark. Edward's shoulders slumped, and in the shadows seemed drained. Percy got up from the chaise he was on, throwing back a quilt and climbing to his feet. He was dressed again, and Percy smiled, thinking that were more times he was mysteriously clothed than he could remember. He tended to pass out after an orgasm, and Percy always ended up back in his clothing or tucked naked into Edward's bed.

Percy went to Edward's side, and Edward looked up with a smile and gathered him into a hug. Edward gave him a kiss, all lips and love. Percy melted and sighed, wrapping his arms around Edward's shoulders and kissing him back.

Edward ended the kiss, dark eyes aglow. Percy tucked his face in Edward's thick hair and breathed him in, loving the masculine scent.

"Mason? How long until that goes up?" Edward asked his brother, who was sitting at the bank of screens and fiddling with equipment Percy barely understood.

"About an hour," Mason replied absentminded.

"Have you heard anything new? How's the reactions out there?" Edward asked, and Percy looked up for Mason's reply, curious as to the answer.

"Day one was disbelief. Everyone thought it was a prank. Palace made the mistake of trying to block it, taking down website after website. But the palace trying so hard to contain it, and ultimately failing, coupled with my earlier videos detailing my imprisonment and torture along with the palace's inability to produce either you or Percy is making the public lean our way."

"How so?" Edward asked, hopeful.

"Well, the major networks are running with it like crazy. Some conservative channels are saying it's a farce, that you and I are the crazy ones, and we've joined some kind of domestic terror society or something and are promoting anti-monarchist views." Mason's voice was full of amusement at that one, and Edward snorted, shaking his head. "But every other network and media organization is of the opinion that we're telling the truth, or most of it. Public opinion on the social media sites are in our favor, too."

"That's good, but I'm still not sure how this will help us," Edward said, pulling Percy into his lap, a hand going to his belly immediately.

"Well, if we to stop and do nothing more, then all it does is piss Father off, destroy our family, and make everyone very, very uncomfortable," Mason quipped, and Percy rolled his eyes.

"Father is king, Mason. This isn't one of those tiny democratic nations that elect their leaders. Father is King by Right of Blood, birthright, and he will not abdicate," Edward said, and Percy looked back and forth between the brothers, listening intently. "None of this matters in the long run."

"Eddie, little brother. Don't you remember your history?"

"I remember plenty, get to the point."

"Once upon a time, in a faraway land named Cassia...."

"Mason!"

"Oh, fine. Farmers have no sense of humor," Mason said to Percy with a wry twist of his sexy mouth. Edward glowered at him. "Not every son or daughter in the line of Airric has been fit to rule. Some were crazy, like our father, some were mentally incompetent, and some were just plain stupid."

"Yes, I am aware."

"So how did they jump succession then, little brother? How did a more worthy royal take the throne? Not counting coup attempts by impatient sons, of course."

"All of the blood princes or princesses in the line of succession would...."

Edward froze under him. Mason leaned back in his chair and laced his hands over his stomach, idly kicking at the floor as the chair swayed back and forth. Mason grinned, and Percy saw Edward swallow, face gone pale.

"What, Edward? What happens?" Percy whispered, worried.

Edward heaved out a shaky breath, and looked at Percy with wide eyes.

"Those of the blood eligible for inheritance convene in the throne room and vote to remove the current monarch from power, there is a challenge to the vote by the monarch, and if the monarch loses then the crown would be passed on to the closest Cassian Royal in the direct succession. That means all blood princes and princesses, which means full-blood siblings of the current monarch and any eligible children of the monarch—they then confront the king, cast their vote of lack of faith… and then the current king can ever accede to their wishes and surrender the crown or…"

"Or?"

"The current monarch faces the presumptive monarch in combat, either by a proxy champion or fighting themselves."

Percy sat still as stone in Edward's lap.

"That means…" Percy whispered. Mason answered him.

"Malcolm is ineligible, and he wouldn't deign to help anyway. I'm ineligible for the same reason as Malcolm. Our sisters are knocked out. Our uncles are deceased, and there are no cousins close enough to the throne to be blood titled. The only blood prince in the line of succession is Edward. That means you, little brother," Mason said, pointing at Edward, "Will need to confront Father in the throne room, list his sins for the world, and cast a single vote for lack of faith. You challenge his right to rule, and he will have to respond. Father will then either have someone else try to kill you, or he'll do it himself."

"Oh my god." Percy couldn't tell if it was either him or Edward who said it in disbelief.

"Then why all this, Mason?!" Edward snapped, arm gesturing wide. "Why drag our family through all this if all I needed was to walk in that room and confront him?"

"Because you can't walk in that room if you're in jail for treason, you fool! It only works in this day and age, in modern times, if the country, if the world, believes your claim of no faith to be true and just. We may not be elected officials, but try ruling a country that calls you usurper instead of king!" Mason shouted as he stood, the chair falling back to the floor, wheels spinning. "If Malcolm isn't disqualified, if I'm not, if our sisters are not tossed out of succession, this doesn't work! They are all too cowed by Father's will to cast a vote of no faith!"

Mason stormed across the small span between them, and Edward stood, gently putting Percy aside. Percy stepped back, out of arm's reach, staring. Reynard, responding to the shouting, ran into the room, eyes alarmed and breathless. Percy backed away some more, and Reynard came to his side.

"I have to prove to the people, to our siblings, to the entire world that Father is truly the monster I've known him to be the whole of our lives. Otherwise you get nowhere near that throne room, and will either die by execution or rot in a cell the rest of your life. He is not fit to rule, and if in the process of freeing us all from his madness I get my revenge, then I will count myself content," Mason whispered, he and Edward's gazes locked, both men bristling with anger and frustration.

"Mason, you ask me to..." Edward began, and Mason nodded once, curt.

"I am asking you to kill him, Edward," Mason agreed. "No mercy for him, he'll only stab you in the back from prison. Kill him, and free us all."

"And if he chooses battle by proxy? Am I to kill a man he's chosen, a man I'm bound to have no quarrel with, and then kill Father?"

"If that comes to pass, and he chooses a proxy then, I will fight in your stead, my prince," Reynard said, stepping forward. "And I will fight the King if that is your choice as well."

Edward nodded at Reynard, not in agreement, but understanding. Edward gripped his shoulder and squeezed, and did the same to Mason.

Percy stared at all three of them, shaking his head. He may not understand entirely what was going on, but the grim resolve on their faces set an iron weight in his gut.

"You are all insane!" Percy whispered loudly, incredulous. He shook his head and walked back to the chaise when they all looked at him, surprised.

CHAPTER ELEVEN

Edward

HE PACED the empty hall, back and forth, the long stretch between the room he and Percy shared and the one shared by his brother and the captain. Reynard had eventually conceded that Lord Estiary's guards were up to the task of protecting them, and had taken to sleeping with Mason in his room instead of skulking about the halls like a spook.

Twenty steps, from door to door, and Edward's strides consumed them before he was ready, and he spun back around, pacing back the way he came, working in his mind over and over the choices laid out before him.

Three weeks since Mason laid out the path to the throne for him, and he was no closer to finding peace with it than he had been that day. Six weeks, almost seven here at Estiary's estate in total. The world was consumed by the scandal devouring the Cassian Dynasty, with public opinion heavily in favor of Edward's claim. Not that he'd made one. It was one thing that he and Mason agreed on in this whole mess—Edward would avoid making a claim of no faith and challenge until he was actually in front of his father. Making a bid now in the court of public opinion would only seed the idea that Edward wanted the throne and this entire debacle was but a smokescreen to hide his greedy bid for power. That didn't stop the more educated of the Cassian public from putting things together themselves and punting about the idea of the no faith challenge. It was trending on all the major social media sites, according to Mason, in the Top 100 topics, and had been for weeks.

He stopped outside his door, and checked on his mate.

Sex was no longer allowed, as Percy was too uncomfortable. Though Edward didn't mind. He was too nervous Percy would go into labor without a doctor to assist. Edward had no experience in human birth—much less that of a male breeder. Edward could deliver a horse or a cow without qualm, but humans left him terrified. He had Mason use Estiary's access to steal everything Heritage had on Percy, and from what he could tell, Percy was ready to give birth any day. Cartwright's estimation on how long Percy's gestation period would be was off, it had to be, because no way was Percy that big and still have another month and change to go. Dr. Rosen, the specialist from the capital, had theorized that Percy could have an even shorter time period than that.

"Pacing again, little brother? This is becoming a nightly occurrence," Mason asked at his shoulder, and Edward jumped. It was the middle of the night, and Mason was in a robe and pajama pants, hair askew. Edward took a deep breath, and took a discreet step back from his brother at the scent of sex and sweat. Not unpleasant, but this was his brother, and that was too weird even for them.

Mason smirked at him as if he knew exactly what he was thinking.

"Yes, I'm pacing again," Edward said to stave off an offensive remark he could see brewing in his brother's eyes. "We need a doctor, one that specializes in breeders. Dr. Rosen is in the capital, and we're eight hundred miles away. I've checked, and while we could always use the doctor that delivered Estiary's babes, he only handled female breeders and I don't know if he's trustworthy. One mention from the man about delivering a male breeder's babe could tip Father off and bring the guards to our doorstep."

"I agree," Mason said, who thankfully didn't offer up any commentary on what else could be bothering Edward. "I could always take Abe and go on a shopping trip."

"For what? You can't buy a doctor with that specialty from a grocery store!" Edward hissed at Mason, annoyed at himself. He could confront a king rabid with anger or plot to overthrow the man's rule, but get he and his brother in the same space and Edward reverted back to being a shy ten year old boy being hassled by his big brother.

"A shopping trip means a kidnapping, my prince," Reynard offered, coming up behind Mason and grabbing his lover about the waist. Edward reached out and carefully closed his bedroom door, ensuring Percy slept undisturbed. It took his mate so long to get back to sleep these days, if he managed to sleep at all.

"Who the hell would you kidnap?" Edward asked, instantly regretting it. "And how many people have you two kidnapped?"

Mason grinned. "The delightful Dr. Rosen, of course. And just a few."

"She's in the capital. And under scrutiny from the palace for corroborating Percy's pregnancy to the press. Do you really think you can get back to the capital, get her and what equipment she needs, and get back here without being caught or seen?"

"We've done far more, in far worse places, with far less than we have now, my prince," Reynard said, calm and unruffled. Mason grinned maniacally at Edward, and he just shook his head and waved a hand at them.

"If I wasn't so desperate for a proper doctor to be on hand for Percy I wouldn't even say yes to this foolishness," Edward muttered, as Mason began to laugh. "Can you do it fast and proper? Get her, and get back here as fast as you can? We've all seen Percy, he's not going to make the full five months."

"Wasn't that number just a guess though?" Reynard said, looking at the door behind which Percy slept on. "Dr. Rosen said it could be four months, or sooner."

"I'm thinking Percy is in the 'sooner' category. His hips have shifted, his back hurts all the time, and the babe is moving. I think he has days left, maybe a week or two at the most."

"Shopping trip!" Mason cheered quietly, and Edward smacked his chest. Mason swatted back at him, and Edward was glad Reynard pulled his brother back out of range or things were about to disintegrate into a brawl.

"We'll leave in an hour, my prince," Reynard said. "Unless you think it's time to move ahead with all of it, and we can all return to the capital."

"Too dangerous," Edward said, shaking his head. "Percy is too close, and I can't confront my father if I'm thinking about Percy going into labor and I'm not there."

Reynard nodded. "Then Mason and I will be off. We have cells now, and they're secure, thanks to our generous host. You will call us if something happens while we are gone, understood?"

"I do, and thank you," Edward said, truly grateful. "How long?"

"We will be back in four days, my prince."

Mason started backing away, dragging Reynard with him. Edward could hear them talking as they returned to their room. Mason's voice was clear before Reynard shut the door.

"Is it kidnapping if the target is willing? Is it just a surprise vacation then?"

Edward laughed, and went back to his sleeping mate, wondering what to tell Percy in the morning when he saw that Reynard and Mason were missing from breakfast.

Percy

PERCY SHIFTED in the chair, glaring at his stomach. He was no longer wearing clothing, just a voluminous bathrobe that covered him chin to toes and made him look twice the size he actually was.

The baby kicked, and Percy groaned, rubbing the spot his little dancer decided should be bruised today. "Little one, please settle. I can't get up again so soon to go to the bathroom, I just don't have it in me," Percy sighed, and thankfully the babe quieted. He picked up his book, and tried reading again. It was a short history of the Cassian Dynasty, the type of books bought by tourists. He was looking for information on the no faith challenge brought to bear by those of the blood, and what he was finding was unsettling.

A no faith challenge had happened only six times in two thousand years. Five of the six were successful, and power exchanged hands from unworthy monarch to worthy successor with a minimum of fuss. Sure, the previous king or queen either died in the challenge or ended up imprisoned for life, but the transition was relatively painless. Those that went to challenge, at least, two of the no faith challenges had resolved by the sitting monarch willingly relinquishing the crown to their successor. Both those cases were in the instances of the monarch being mentally or physically unsuited for rule. One was mentally damaged from a riding incident, and the other rendered sterile from scarlet fever. Both those cases the monarch stepped down, willingly abdicated, and spent their life in opulent splendor outside the capital at a private residence.

The other challenges resulted in the proxy combatant either dying in the challenge or the monarch themselves dying, or with the monarch losing the match but not their life, and going to prison. It turned out a few in the Dynasty had gone legitimately mad, and were a danger to everyone and themselves.

The last challenge is what worried Percy the most. It was startlingly similar to the situation they were in now. A king two hundred years ago had killed his Queen for a suspected infidelity, and in the days after the murder the sons and daughters, mourning the life of their mother, had brought to the king a no faith challenge. The king, in a rage, had fought his eldest son, the current crown prince in combat. The father killed his heir and son, winning the challenge.

The king then had skipped the two next oldest blood heirs,

and made the youngest, a lad of thirteen, into his heir. The boy was spared his father's revenge due to his age, while the king imprisoned his two other remaining children for life, charged with treason. They died in prison less than ten years after being incarcerated.

Percy tossed the book aside, and pushed up on the arms of the chair, trying to settle his hips better. He was always in pain. Dull aches as his body rapidly changed to support the little one he carried, and while he begrudged his babe nothing, the discomfort of being this pregnant left him fitful and constantly uncomfortable. His hips and back hurt the most, and if he moved after too long sitting still, they popped and creaked, alternating between relief and pain.

The door opened, and Percy looked up hopefully, but it was just Edward and Lord Lucius. Percy slumped, wishing it was Mason and Reynard with the doctor. It was evening on the fourth day since they left, and Percy trusted Reynard and Mason to return, but he wished they would hurry up. He wanted to have this baby, and now. Edward saw his pout and gave him a sympathetic smile, walking to his chair and talking his hand.

"How do you feel, Percy?"

"Fat and sore," Percy snapped, and instantly felt bad. He looked up at Edward, but his mate merely smiled at him and patted his hand. "I'm sorry, Edward."

"No need to be sorry. It's my fault you're pregnant, after all," Edward told him, sitting on the coffee table nearby and lifting Percy's feet to his lap. Percy gave a happy moan as Edward rubbed his feet, soothing the aches.

"It is your fault," Percy agreed, with a blush sweeping across his cheeks. Edward smiled back at him, his strong hands so firm and in control that Percy wanted him and badly in that moment. Edward's eyes, always so dark, held a fire when his desire was roused, and the way they traced over his legs, his hips, even the mountain of his stomach told Percy that his mate and master wanted him. "I want to have the baby. I want to..."

Edward chuckled, his hands moving up his ankles to massage his calves. Percy was ready to melt into the armchair. Edward learned forward, and whispered to him, "I know what you want, little one. It's been too long. You need to be under me, legs spread wide, tight little hole full of cock and cum. I want to hear you panting in desire, your body sucking me deeper, demanding I fill you with my seed. Is that what you want?"

Percy nodded, mouth parting as he breathed faster, eyes locked on Edward. His prince gave him a wicked smile, and whispered, "Perhaps I'll put you on your hands and knees, and spread your pert little ass apart, so I can see that tight, pink hole clench for me. Wet and hot, and so needy. I'll open you, get you ready for me, and then I'll mount you like a stallion does a mare, hard and rough and wild. Does that sound better?"

Percy could only nod, slowly, eyes wide, chest rising and falling rapidly as his whole body went up in flames. Percy whimpered, and his cock twitched, highly interested in the images Edward generated. His hole clenched and grew damp, and Percy was ready to beg Edward to fuck him or kill his mate—he was too pregnant to be this horny. Percy glared at Edward, and his mate chuckled, dark eyes bright with passion, and he leaned back, an innocent expression on his handsome features.

"Such charming domesticity," Lord Lucius said, observing them from the small table next to the window, the setting sun casting a red glow over the man's silver hair. Percy realized the older man must have heard his master, and he blushed even harder, face red and burning.

"Anything interesting happening in the capital, Lucius?" Edward called over his shoulder, hands rubbing Percy's feet again. He relaxed into Edward's touch, body still humming with arousal but without the edge. "Hopefully no kidnappings to report, no additional manhunts?"

"Not that I can tell, no," Lord Lucius replied, looking down at a thin tablet on the table, finger gliding over the screen. "Your sisters are still languishing in the country, your brother Malcolm is still at the palace, and your two sisters by marriage are....well, that is interesting."

"What?" Edward asked, twisting on the coffee table to see Lord Lucius better.

"The Queen-presumptive hasn't been seen in public since Mason's escape. Princess Camilla, Mason's horrible wife, has been seen multiple times, mostly with the king. Disgusting, but then there's no accounting for taste.... Here it is..." Lord Lucius began to read off the tablet. "Princess Arianna was seen this morning in the windows of the royal nursery, photographed by a paparazzi using long-range lenses. The princess appeared to be several pounds thinner, haggard in appearance, and from the image looks to be severely ill. Theories abound that this potential illness is why she has yet to be seen in public since Prince Mason's historic exit from the capital.'"

"Edward!" Percy cried out as Edward got to his feet, striding to the table where their host sat. Lord Lucius turned the tablet, and Edward froze at the image there. Even Percy could see it from where he sat.

Arianna was thin, ill-thin, and her hair was lank and dull. The image was distorted through distance and the window pane, but even Percy could tell that all was not well with Princess Arianna.

"Saint's blood! What has he done to her?" Edward cursed under his breath, rigid with anger.

"Mason said she stayed behind for her children's sake—that she refused to leave them. If she angered the king, who knows what he's done to her," Lord Lucius mused, reaching for his ever-present goblet of wine. "She helped Mason escape, and found out the truth about her children. Such a thing is bound to enrage any woman, even one like her. Perhaps her condition is the result of a confrontation between her and the king."

"He struck me for defiance, he tried to choke Percy to death, he beat and tortured Mason for days—what has he done to Ari?" Edward backed away from the tablet, and in his eyes Percy could see anger, frustration, even guilt. There were nightmarish possibilities for what a madman could do to a vulnerable woman, and Percy could see each hit home in his master's heart.

"This is not your fault!" Percy cried, startling Edward into looking at him. "None of this is your fault. I see you thinking it! Stop it!"

Edward stared at him, shocked. Even Lord Lucius was startled. Percy ignored the noble in favor of his prince. "Don't you dare think you could have stopped this, or prevented it!

This is all on King Henry's shoulders, and none of this is your fault!"

Percy was panting, and he struggled to sit up more, and he ignored the sharp twinge in his hips and back. Edward hurried to his side, hands outstretched to help him. Percy got to his feet, swaying, and Edward gathered him close.

"Don't you dare take any more guilt or grief on that isn't yours to begin with," Percy hissed at his prince, who gave him a thorough, searching glance, and nodded once. Edward appeared sheepish, and he gave Percy a small smile, the vulnerability in that tiny moment enough to cool his annoyance. Percy frowned, but he nodded back, pleased. "Good. Now help me to the bathroom, I need to pee."

Edward chuckled, "Yes, my love."

Edward made Percy's heart hurt in the most delicious way when he swept him up into his arms, Percy's greater weight nothing to the strength of his mate. Percy hugged him around his neck and kissed his cheek, and Edward carried him to the bathroom to pee for what felt like the millionth time.

Edward

EDWARD WAITED patiently outside the bathroom in the hall, watching as the sun set behind the forest he could see through the ceiling high windows lining the hallway. The lamps scattered about the gardens came on in seconds, and Edward could see Lord Lucius' black-clad guards patrolling in the lights. Percy was in the bathroom, and he could hear his little mate muttering as he went about his business.

Pregnancy may not make Percy comfortable, but it was doing something for his personality. Percy still wasn't the most talkative of people, preferring silence and a watchful attitude to in depth conversation, but he was coming out of his shell by leaps and bounds. If his new-found courage and the lessening in his crippling shyness was a result of his pregnancy and evaporated after the babe's birth Edward would be fine with it, but part of him wished for his mate's sake that some of it would remain. Percy spent too much of his life before Edward afraid and nervous; Edward would see his mate embrace his courage and enjoy life to the fullest.

Edward frowned when he heard nothing from the bathroom. Usually Percy would call him back when he was done so he could help him from the bathroom. Edward walked to the door and knocked, "Little one? Percy?"

Silence. "Percy!"

"Edward…" at that tentative call, Edward slammed through the door, and went to the stall. He opened it, and saw Percy standing, leaning against the inner wall.

"What's wrong, little one?" Edward asked, reaching for Percy, his robe askew and falling from a shoulder, revealing Percy's gravid and naked body underneath.

Edward grabbed the robe, and his hand came away wet. The robe was soaked in a clear, viscous fluid, and he was about to ask what it was when realization hit. He stopped, staring, and a heavy, musky aroma filled his senses. Percy whimpered, and Edward watched in awe and terror as his mate's abdomen rippled.

A contraction. Percy was in labor.

CHAPTER TWELVE

Percy

THE PAIN wasn't too bad. It forced its way across his abdomen and hips, and his lower back ached horribly, but it wasn't too much to bear.

The shock on Edward's face was scary, though. "Edward!"

Edward jerked, and came back to himself. One arm went around Percy under his arms, and Edward picked him up and lifted him from the stall, and the unfortunate puddle he left when his body decided to flush his rectum in preparation for birth. It had been startling, and uncomfortable, but the rapid displacement of waste from his rectum and the clear, clean fluid that followed in the second wave told Percy that these were no false contractions—he was in labor.

Edward let him lean against the sink, arm still holding him upright, and with his free hand his prince pulled out his cell and dialed.

"Answer, c'mon, answer dammit..." Edward muttered, and Percy could hear it ring and ring. It clicked over to voicemail, and Edward growled in frustration but left a message. "Percy is in labor. Get back here, and now!"

Pain made Percy gasp, grasping at Edward. He felt lightheaded, and his wavered on his feet. "Percy!"

Edward picked him up in his arms, and Percy moaned,

feeling nauseous. "I don't like this so much, Edward."

"Me neither. Let's get you in bed, okay?" Edward said, walking them out of the bathroom and down the hall.

Edward's long strides carried them past the room they were just in, and Lord Lucius saw them as they passed. "Prince Edward!"

"No time, Lucius!" Edward called over his shoulder. The noble appeared in the door behind them, and followed at a fast walk.

Another contraction was coming. It built, tightening, moving his insides around, and the baby woke in a flurry of movement. "Oh! She doesn't like it much either."

Edward took the stairs, the stone steps echoing as Edward climbed, sure-footed despite the panic Percy could see hovering in his eyes. "She, huh? So you agree with Mason?"

"I don't know for sure," Percy said, gasping as his body tried to twist itself out of Edward's arms. Edward tightened his grip, making the second floor and walking them down the hall to their room. Lord Lucius had caught up, and was on his cell, presumably talking to his few, actual servants. Lord Lucius had a housekeeper, a small army of maids, a single stable master after the unfortunate removal of the first one, and a dozen trained and lethal guards, and not counting the small harem of pleasure slaves he kept.

"I like the idea of a little girl," Percy said, one hand on his abdomen. The muscles under his hand were rippling, in a wholly unconscious manner that left him disturbed and excited. His body was moving ahead with the birth regardless of whether or not Percy was ready. That thought scared him and reassured him simultaneously.

"A healthy baby and a healthy consort are all I want right now," Edward said, sweeping into their room and heading for the king-sized bed.

A burst of activity behind them made Percy look up, and a handful of maids came in the room, carrying fresh linens and blankets. Edward stepped back as they remade the bed, pulling back the blankets and piling pillows high. Edward laid him down, sitting up, and removed the soaked robe from his shoulders. Percy grimaced, and he realized another small flood of fluid had dampened the fabric. Edward saw his problem, and sat on the side of the bed, a clean washcloth in his hand. Percy suffered through his mate cleaning him, and his face burned.

Edward pulled a sheet high over his belly, and Percy clutched it, glad to be hidden from the curious eyes of the maids. Edward waved a hand, and they fled just as fast as they appeared.

"How are you feeling?" Edward asked him, rubbing a hand over his belly.

"The contractions are far apart, and don't hurt too badly," Percy said, even as he could feel his belly tighten for another round. "I need a towel under me, Edward, please."

Edward was quick to comply, slipping a thick, fluffy towel under his ass. Percy shifted, and he found himself wishing he could stand. This was too stifling, laying back. "What do you need, Percy?"

"I want to...help me up," Percy sobbed, sweating, a contraction tackling him. He cried out, gasping for air, the immense tightening of muscles in his core startling and inescapable. "Edward, this is going to be fast and I don't know what I'm doing!"

Percy rolled to his side, and Edward was there, helping him to his knees. Percy knelt on the bed, knees wide, the towel under him. Fluid dripped in an increasing stream from his ass, and he could feel himself opening, stretching. "Edward!"

A contraction made him arch his back, screaming. He had no strength in his legs, and Edward tried to pull him flat to his back. Percy fought him, and Edward relented, helping Percy stay up on his knees on the bed. For some reason his body wanted to be upright. He wasn't going to be birthing this babe flat on his back like a female breeder. The sheet pooled on the bed, and Percy was left naked and bare, but his body's single-minded determination to give birth made him forget about being embarrassed.

"Percy? Dear God, Mason and Reynard need to hurry up!"

"I need you to...Edward, you're going to be delivering our baby." Percy was breathing through the waves of pain, slumping as the contraction eased its grip on his body. "They aren't going to make it."

"I tried calling them as well," Lord Lucius said, standing politely in the doorway, the usually reserved and sarcastic noble appearing hesitant, nervous. "I got no reply. Should I call for my doctor, Prince Edward?"

"Percy? Up to you. I've delivered horses before, but I have no idea how to deliver a human baby. I'm sure the mechanics are similar..." Edward asked him, as Percy held on to Edward, his prince holding him upright.

Another wave was coming. Hot fluid poured from his ass. It was thick, so it wasn't blood, and Percy's eyes went wide as he felt his insides opening, dilating. It was extremely disturbing and enlightening. His body was moving ahead with the birth, and Percy's nerves be damned. Percy clawed at Edward's arms, lifting himself up higher on his knees, the inside of his thighs soaking wet.

Edward was saying something to Lord Lucius, but Percy was past hearing anything but his body's demands. Soon. So very soon, he would be holding his babe.

Percy's eyes shut against a strong wave of pain, and he cried out, jaw aching from clenching his teeth. The wave came and crested, holding for heartbeats, then eased. Percy tried pushing with it, but nothing happened. Too soon to push yet, and he relaxed.

He opened his eyes, just in time for the lights to go out.

Glass shattered nearby, and Edward went still beside him.

"What the devil is going on…?" Lord Lucius said at the doorway, and Percy watched as the noble turned to the hall. There was still enough light in the deepening twilight to see, the moon rising, its glow dim but filling the hall.

A shadow coalesced in the deeper darkness of the hall, solid black and tall. Percy cried out in alarm as the shadow moved, and Lord Lucius fell to the floor. "Edward!"

Edward

HIS HEART stopped when the lights went out. Before he even heard the glass shatter down the hall, he knew.

His father had found them, and they were out of time.

Lucius fell, crumpled to the floor. Edward threw himself

in front of Percy as the shadow at the door raised an arm, the gun firing. Flashes from the muzzle illuminated a man covered in black from head to toes, a semi-automatic weapon aimed right for him.

The nanosecond it took him to understand the gun was aimed at him, and not Percy, was all it took for Percy to see the same. His mate screamed, and lurched to the side, pushing Edward back. The gun fired, three shots, the whole of the world slowed in a horrible tableau. The bullets ripped through the air between them, and Edward's heart stopped when he saw Percy jerk.

A swath of red bloomed in his side, and Percy stared up at him, ice-blue eyes wide in fear and pain. Edward caught Percy as he toppled to the bed, laying him on his side. Movement in the doorway made him look, and the gunman walked in the room, stepping over Lucius where he lay on the floor.

Rage unlike anything he'd ever felt swept over him. Edward screamed, and sprang to his feet. He charged the armed man, who wasn't expecting it at all by the way he fumbled to aim at Edward. Edward poured his fear and horror into his rush, and he tackled the gunman, crashing them back out into the hall.

They smashed into the far wall, glass breaking, the window behind the gunman shattering, great showering lengths of razor-sharp shards cascading down on top of them. Edward wrapped his hands around the weapon, even as it fired wildly, shooting into the ceiling. Pain exploded along his shoulders and back, and Edward rolled away from the still falling glass.

Screams and shouting filled the hall. The gunman, clothing ripped by glass and covered in blood, roared in anger and towered above Edward, the gun missing but a long shard of glass in his hand. Edward kicked out, and hit the man square in the chest, arm raised to stab him where he lay on the floor. The man flew backward, and Edward scrambled to his feet.

They faced each other in the darkness, the shifting clouds in the sky hiding the rising moon, taking and giving away light as they circled. Edward fell into a defensive crouch, so very glad he had asked Reynard for lessons. He was no expert, and still lost to the captain every time, but by the Saints, he was going to save Percy and their babe if it was the last thing he did.

The man lunged, stabbing ahead with the blade of glass. Edward stepped forward, dodging the blow, and caught the man's wrist, and brought his other hand down and smacked his opponent's elbow. A pop, and the glass fell to the floor. The man screamed, but swung again with his other arm. Edward stepped forward again, and sent his knee up, slamming it into the other man's groin. The man's blow landed, but Edward was all instinct and thought was gone—he attacked with total purpose, to protect his mate.

Edward kept moving, pushing ahead, fist smashing into the cloth covered face, and he kicked the man backwards with a blow to his stomach. The man stumbled back, arms flailing, and Edward was about to follow when another shadow moved behind his opponent.

An arm snaked around the gunman's throat, and a vicious boot to the back of his knee took him to the floor. The arm tightened, and there was sickening, wet snap, and the attacker's body went limp.

Mason let the body drop at his feet. "Hey, Eddie, not bad.

Keep your hands up next time."

Percy

"EDWARD! EDWARD, no!" Percy screamed, as his mate and the stranger crashed back into the hall. He tried to get up, to follow, but his body refused to cooperate.

Percy fell back to the bed, his side slick with blood, Percy screamed, a contraction ripping through his body, and the wound on his side bloomed in agony. Blood ran from the bullet hole, and Percy slapped a hand over it, his legs pushing him back up to his knees, he was sweating profusely, body wracked by fine tremors, but he had a baby to deliver and he wasn't going to fail.

The sounds coming in from the hall were horrible. Screams, shouts, the sound of flesh hitting flesh, and the crashing of glass all made Percy desperate to see what was happening. He grabbed the headboard, and used it to hold himself up as he kept his other hand over the wound in his side. It was high, and near his bottom rib on the left side. It hit the top swell of his baby bump, but Percy could feel the child moving, lower in his womb, and he hoped that if the babe was hit as well, she could make it until he birthed her. She couldn't be helped until he got her out.

A contraction came again, hitting out of nowhere. His fingers creaked as he clutched the headboard, sweating running down his body, and a gush of fluid was expelled, hot and thick, and the smell of warm flesh and blood was sickening. Whether this was normal or not it didn't matter—Percy felt blood gush out of the bullet wound, the contraction forcing it to pump under his hand despite the pressure he was applying. His hand slipped, and more blood ran down his side.

It was happening. Even as his head spun, and black pots danced in front of his eyes, Percy could feel his body opening further. He pushed, straining, screaming, as a contraction crested.

Edward

HE SPRINTED for the bedroom, Percy's screams freezing his blood. He ran into the room and jumped over the man on the floor, and dashed to the bed in time to catch Percy as he fell over.

Blood ran down his entire left side. Blood stained the sheets, from the injury and from between his legs. Edward was about to lay him down when a slim hand reached out and stopped him.

"No! The male breeder births upright! Move him out of the blood, and hold him up!" Dr. Rosen told him, her orders clear and to the point. Edward did as she commanded, climbing over the bed, holding Percy up, out of the mess on the sheets. Edward crawled and pulled, and managed to get Percy upright and on his knees. Percy was moaning, eyes fluttering, barely conscious. Dr. Rosen crawled on the bed beside, him, snapping orders as she slapped a bandage over the wound in Percy's side.

"Get the power back on now—we need light! Someone check the nobleman on the floor, make sure he's alive. If he's dead, get him out of the way. If he's alive do the same, I'll tend to him after I help Percy. Move it!" Dr. Rosen snapped out, and Mason and Reynard obeyed with alacrity.

Lucius was dragged to the side, but Edward couldn't tell if he was alive or not. He couldn't care. Callous, but Percy was waking in his arms. Reynard ran out of the room, as Mason came back from dragging Lucius out into the hall.

"Edward..." Percy sighed, ice-blue eyes wet with tears, sweat beading on his face.

"Little one," Edward whispered, swallowing. Percy's body bowed in his arms, and Edward could feel the tremendous effort put forth by each contraction. "Stay strong, stay awake for me."

Mason was at Edward's side, staring down at Percy as blood soaked the bandage and the small man gasped in pain. Dr. Rosen was behind Percy, gloves on, and she was checking between his mate's legs.

"The baby is in the birth canal. I can't tell if the baby was hit by the bullet, there's more blood coming out from the uterus than there should be. Was he bleeding before he got shot?" She asked, sitting up, blonde hair mused and her clothes stained by blood.

"No, he wasn't," Edward answered, heart sinking. "The fluid was clear, slightly pinkish, and thick. No blood."

"Okay, that means the uterus was punctured by the bullet. We need to deliver, and now, before he bleeds out."

"C-Section?" Mason asked, and Edward hoped not. Percy would lose too much blood.

"No, the baby is already presenting, it's too late. Mason! Get those lights back on. Go help Reynard!" Dr. Rosen ordered, and Mason backed out of the room, face bone white and eyes haunted. Edward nodded to his brother, and Mason left, closing the door behind him.

"Edward, I love you," Percy sighed, tears running from the corners of his eyes.

"I love you, too. Now stay awake for me."

"I will. Want to hold my baby," Percy trembled, and Edward could feel his body gathering for another contraction.

Dr. Rosen slid from the bed and ran to her bag, dropped by the door when she entered. She grabbed her gear, and came back to the bed, opening it and pulling out the contents.

Percy's contraction bowled through his body like a tidal wave, and his small mate pushed. "Percy, should you be pushing?"

"Yes! Percy, push! You're minutes away, don't stop!" Dr. Rosen ordered as she climbed back on the bed. "Prince Edward, hold him high, and don't let go."

"I won't. I'll never let go," Edward vowed to Percy, as Dr. Rosen got behind Percy, dragging her gear with her, medical equipment ready. He had no idea what any of that stuff was, and he was too absorbed by the man in his arms to care.

Percy pushed again, the contractions closer, more urgent, and Edward knew it was almost over. Percy was pale, sweating, and his head fell back on his shoulders as he arched into the contraction. Blood dripped down Percy's side, rivulets staining his hip and thigh.

"Percy, push hard on the next wave! Almost done!" Dr. Rosen ordered, and Percy obeyed, pushing.

Edward waited, as Percy bled all over him and the bed, and their child fought to be born.

EPILOGUE

Mason

THEY RAN back up the stairs, Reynard at his side. The generator in the basement was on, and they shut off the power to rest of the house but for the wing where Edward and Percy had their bedroom. Reynard had his gun out and up, in a ready position as they ran down the hall, sweeping the shadows.

There was no other sign of intruders, but for the dead man on the floor. Reynard believed it was a single assassin, sent to take out Edward as soon as he was vulnerable. Percy going into labor merely provided the assassin the distraction he need to get inside the mansion. The main fuse box was disabled, fuses torn out and missing, but they were able to get the generators up and running, bypassing the main panel.

Lucius was awake, leaning on the wall by Edward's door. They ran down the hall, boots cracking over the shattered glass, broken from Edward's fight with the assassin.

"Luke, is everyone alright? What's happening?" Mason asked, as Reynard went to investigate the bedrooms on either side of Edward's. "Where are the guards, dammit?"

"They're securing the property, doing a sweep to see if there any more killers on their way. They've found a single unmarked SUV a mile away out near the main drive. There's baby formula inside, and diapers. Medical supplies." Luke met his eyes, and Mason was going to be sick.

"He was going to kill Eddie and Percy, and take the baby," Mason breathed out, fighting back bile.

"I think so, yes," Luke agreed, holding a hand to his head. He had a cut along his hairline, and spectacular bruising. "I poked my head in the room, but the beautiful doctor ordered me out. Said she'd call if she needed assistance."

"What's happening? Is Percy okay? You said he was shot," Reynard came back, shrugging off his jacket so his holster under his left arm was more accessible. He put his gun in the holster, but left it unsnapped for easier drawing.

"I don't know," Mason replied, and he shook head to toe. They were almost too late. Any longer getting back from the capital with Dr. Rosen and it would have been a nightmare. Edward may have been able to defeat the assassin without Mason's help, but none of them here had serious medical training, and helping a male breeder deliver after being shot was beyond them all.

They all went quiet, staring at the door.

Minutes passed. Eternity came and went.

Screams ripped apart the expectant silence.

The three of them jumped at the cry, and Lucius gripped Mason's shoulder, trying to comfort him. He was too tired to pace, and Mason winced when Percy cried out in pain again, thinner, less volume.

Weaker.

Mason let the tears come. For Edward, for Percy, for the baby in that room who hadn't had a chance to live yet.

"Please, let them live," Mason whispered, eyes drawn tight, sweat dripping down his face to blend with his tears of frustration and fear. "Please, by the grace of the Saints and the Blood of Our Line, let them live...."

A wail, thin and hopeless. Reynard swore viciously and spun, punching the wall, the sound of something breaking filling the empty quiet that fell just as suddenly. Lucius barely reacted, swallowing, and Mason grew taut as cable, and vibrated in horrific tension. Two of the three people he loved most in this world were in there now, fighting to bring a fourth into the world.

Mason spun away from the door, and went to the destroyed window, the moon fully risen now and shining her silver light down across the luxurious grounds. Reynard came to his side and embraced him, and they waited, tense and nervous.

The door behind them creaked open, a bare sliver of light spilling into the darkness where they waited. Mason spun, tottering as he almost fell over, and he anxiously approached the light, hoping even as he despaired. Luke watched impassively, accepting of whatever outcome. Reynard gripped his shoulder, keeping him upright.

"Are they..." he swallowed, and tried again, asking the form standing in the doorway, the light haloed behind the figure making features impossible to discern.

"Edward, is Percy...Is Percy alive? The baby?"

The door swung open, wider, revealing Edward. He was pale and bloody, eyes wide and pouring tears. They could see the bed behind him, sheets stained by blood, Dr. Rosen working at Percy's side.

"Mason," Edward said, and Mason tore his eyes away from Percy to see his little brother in front of him, holding a towel-wrapped bundle. "Mason, hold her while I go back to Percy.

Dr. Rosen needs to stop the bleeding. Reynard, go in please, she needs someone with medical training."

Reynard went, a single glance down at the squirming towel Edward held before slipping past into the room. Edward held out his arms, and Mason automatically responded, taking the tiny, wrinkled, whimpering babe from his brother. Edward backed away, and returned to Percy's side.

Mason held her gently, his big arms feeling awkward and too hard as he cradled her as gently as he could to his chest. She stared back up at him, and he stepped forward just enough for the light in the room to illuminate her face.

A dark shock of ink black hair covered her head, and she was pretty, even for a babe minutes old. She stared up at him from a face that could only be Edward's, but delicate and ethereal.

When she scrunched up her cupid's bow lips and sucked in a great gust of air, letting loose a shrill cry, Mason laughed. Her ice-blue eyes were angry, and she appeared so fussed about being born in such an improper manner as during an assassination attempt. He fell in love with his newborn niece as she screamed bloody murder at the top of her lungs.

"Hello, niece of mine," Mason whispered to the tiny babe in his arms, gently touching her button nose with a fingertip. "Looks like I was right."

Percy

SHE WAS perfect. Ten toes, ten fingers, thick head of hair that Dr. Rosen said would fall out then grow back in. She was perfect, and beautiful, and she felt amazing in his arms. She looked just like Edward, but for one tiny detail.

She had his eyes. Ice-blue and crystalline pure.

"Percy!" Edward scolded as he came in the room, carrying a tray with their breakfast on it. Percy had eggs and toast, and the baby had formula. "Dr. Rosen said you could only hold her if you had someone with you, so you didn't tear your stitches."

Percy chuckled and shook his head. He was fine. He saw the bottle, and waited for Edward to get closer.

For one horrible moment Percy's heart broke that he could not nurse his babe, but his body didn't produce milk. Breeders were never designed to rear their young; they were separated immediately at birth, and so a breeder had no need for functional mammary glands. He rallied though as he sat up, holding her securely in the crook of his arm. She fit there perfectly as well, tiny and adorable.

His heart hurt just looking at her. Never in all his dreams did he ever truly dare to hope for this day. The day that he could hold his babe, his child, and never fear that her father would steal her away, leaving him broken and destroyed. Percy thanked Fate and the Universe again for bringing him Edward. Without his prince, none of this would be possible.

Edward settled the tray over his legs, and sat beside him on the bed. It was two days since he delivered, and he was feeling better every hour. His body was recovering from the birthing faster than the bullet wound, and Edward was amazed at his progress. Percy took the bottle from the tray, testing the temperature as the good doctor showed him, and held it up to his daughter's lips. She latched on, and began suckling with impressive strength. She was Edward's daughter all right.

Edward help a small piece of toast up, and Percy nibbled on it as he fed his baby. She had taken to the bottle instantly, without any trouble, impressing the doctor.

Percy was gazing down at her as Mason and Reynard came in, walking to where Edward sat and staring down at him and the baby. Mason winked at Percy, and grinned. Reynard gave him an awed smile, and went back to staring at his daughter, and Percy could tell the captain was as swayed as they all were by her charms.

"Is the car ready?" Edward asked, and Mason nodded.

"We'll be able to head out to the capital once everyone is done eating," Mason said, his smile disappearing.

It was time. Edward and Mason were heading back to the capital. Mason had posted video of Percy shortly after he gave birth, the wound in his side covered in blood-stained bandages, the bed beneath him soaked. Percy had been unconscious, and looked to be near death in the video. Mason had then shown the dead assassin, and the short message at the end made it clear who was responsible.

"...My father sent a killer to murder myself and my consort, and then steal our babe from Percy's womb. I am Edward, Prince of the Blood. I am coming for you, Father. It's time you answered for your crimes against our family."

Reynard would be taking Percy and the baby to safety. It was decided that Mason would fight for Edward as proxy depending on what choice the king came to once Edward delivered his no faith challenge. The whole country was going wild, crowds around the palace by the thousands, all waiting to catch a glimpse of Edward as he returned to the capital to challenge his father.

"Percy?" Edward asked him, and he looked up from his child, realizing he'd fallen into a daze just watching her eat.

"Hmm?"

"Have you settled on a name?" Edward asked him, and Percy smiled as the others perked up, paying attention.

"I have." Percy smiled at his lover, and Edward nodded at him with encouragement.

Percy waited, and Mason shifted with impatience. Reynard merely smiled at him.

"It is my pleasure to present to you, father and gentlemen, Her Royal Highness Princess Penelope of Cassia. To her family though, I think she'll just be Penny."

Edward smiled, dark eyes full of love and promise. His mate leaned over, and pressed a kiss to his forehead, before pulling back and pressing a kiss to his lips.

Percy kissed Edward back, happy and content. He had his child, his mate, and his friends. The future was still uncertain, and full of danger, but there was hope in every beginning, and Percy's heart was full of love.

End

TO BE CONTINUED

The adventures of Percy, Edward and their family will continue in BOOK FOUR of the Bred For Love Series.

Look for it in Spring of 2016.

Thank you for reading! And don't forget to leave a review for the author!

ABOUT THE AUTHOR

Revella Hawthorne is the pen name of a slightly weird thirty something woman who loves her pets, her books, and writing of course! She works for everyone's least favorite uncle by day and her inner deviance is set free at night, usually ending up typed out in delightful detail on her stressed out computer.

Revella has been writing since she was a teenager, and it wasn't until a pretty serious life-changing event rolled through her daily grind that she decided to publish her own erotica stories. She also specializes in fanfiction, under the name of Revella on the Fanfiction.net website.

Her current project is a collection of novellas in the *Bred for Love Series*, and the next part of Edward and Percy's journey is coming Spring 2016

OTHER BOOKS BY REVELLA HAWTHORNE

BRED FOR LOVE SERIES
    The Prince's Consort
    The King's Command
    A Royal Rebellion

Made in the USA
San Bernardino, CA
20 November 2016